A BL

A BLACK MAN'S PAIN

By

Teresa Mason Browning

This book is a work of fiction. Places, events, and situations in this story are purely fictional. Any resemblance to actual persons, living or dead are coincidental.

Published by Create Space 11/17/2014

ISBN: 1503246213 (e-book)

ISBN: 978-1503246218 (Paperback)

This book is printed on acid free paper.

Printed in Amerrique

Author's Note

To the Creator above, thanks for instilling in me a mind to keep dreaming and producing work that you are pleased with. I do nothing without keeping you first and foremost in my life.

This book took me by storm! It came at a time in my life where I was going through something very personal; something that took me to the very edge of life where I thought I wouldn't make it. As I lay in bed I said, "Lord, if you help me get up, I will finish the work you set out for me to complete." My help came and I am standing on my word.

I want to give a special thanks to Everette Spigner. Without him there would be no "A Black Man's Pain." He shared his story with me and allowed me to share it with the world.

My hat goes off to the team that continues to put up with me even though sometimes I get beside myself, (act a donkey). Brenda Means and The Gaurdian; these two editors/friends are an awesome duo. What one can't find the other would share.

Special shout out to Sister Pam Morgan for keeping me grounded. To my sister in the gospel and my Bestie in the South, Drusilla Weathers. Thank you! You know why. To my sister Lady Whitney who still sits behind the Gates of Hell (prison). To my God sister Joyce Davis for extending a hand when I really needed help. To my two home girls Marcia Page Conyers and Jaqueline Koko Parrish, you two are the best friend/sisters a woman could have. To my awesome nephew Marcus always smiling Means. Thanks for being there and listening.

To my children Tanisha, Latriece, Jose, TyHisha and Thomas; my world is complete because I have you and the Creator. Although we are apart, my heart never stops wishing and holding on to faith that He will allow all of us to one day be together again. Not one day shall pass where I don't say, I love you. To my grandchildren James, Jaida, and Jasiah; Nanna loves you more than life itself.

To my Special Friend Odel Robinson; you have shown me a man can love a woman and treat her with grace. Loving you has been one of the best things to ever happen to me.

Thank you for being there for me and encouraging me to keep my head up and reach the unreachable dreams.

A Black Man's Pain

Prologue spirit

Who says a man's spirit can't be broken? Take the time to look around as you go about your day; slow down and gaze into the eyes of the countless men who pass you by. Tell me, what do you see deep within, happiness or pain? Now, look into the mirror at the pain inside yourself and imagine piling all of it on top of theirs; it's your past but they're the ones you punish.

I learned the true meaning of one man's pain. I searched his eyes time and time again to find the endless hurt he held inside. People are quick to speak of a woman's suffering, but sometimes the shoe is on the other foot. Men are just like women, faithful, loyal and supportive of their families. The same is also true for men who bear the hurt and pain dished out by their indigenous queens. So, what would happen if the tables were turned, and he was mistreated because of what someone else had done to you in your past? Would he be another statistic, a pressure point snapped, broken and lashing out? Or, would he be a real man, led by his heart to release and forgive?

Ervin's story begins in his birthplace of Columbia, SC. A strong black man, great son, good father and loving husband, who hides the scars of years of abuse, hurt, rejection and separation; the majority of which comes from the women he should be able to count on the most.

Chapter 1

For the first five years of my existence, Mom's crazy lifestyle sent me packing to my Grandparents. I was a "bastard," but when I asked what that meant no one seemed able explain it to me. All I knew was that my Grandparents gave me plenty of unconditional love. Being so young I didn't know what any of this meant, or the effect this sense of rejection would have on me when I grew up.

It was the beginning of a journey down a hard and lonely road.

In the beginning my life was absolutely wonderful. My Grandparents gave me pretty much everything a little boy could ever want growing up and Grandma's food was off the chain. Me and Grandpa would always be on the floor playing with my toys, or just goofing off and making all kinds of noise till Grandma couldn't take anymore and put us out the house. That's when Grandpa would show me how to sneak over to the window and grab cookies and slices of cake without Grandma seeing us. Even though I thought we were getting away with it every time, Grandma knew what we were up to. We knew this because every once in a while she would put two glasses of milk in the window for us. Grandpa always said it was the magic cake fairy and she wanted to make sure we had something to wash the cake down with.

Grandma would give me a bath and read to me most nights when she wasn't tired. I loved the quality time that both Grandparents spent with me. They showed me how to pick up after myself, taught me how to write my name and even showed me how to count. I remember those days like yesterday.

At certain times, I heard my Grandma talking to Grandpa about some other lady she was calling my mom and something about her goings and comings. I always thought my Grandma was my mom but who was this other lady she was talking about? One day I decided to ask Grandma what she was talking about and who was this other lady she was calling my mom.

Grandma said, "Ervin how long have you been behind that chair listening to me?"

I said, "I was just playin and heard you telling Grandpa about the lady you call my momma. You not my momma Grandma?"

"Ervin baby, come over here and sit down with me. I'll tell you all about your momma."

Grandma told me about how my mom grew up in the very house we were in and her room was the room I was staying in. She told me all about her being in the top of her class in school, about her winning the school spelling bee four times in a row, and; she was a cheerleader in high school and how she graduated with honors. Grandma told me that she grew up to be a very beautiful woman and that sometimes beautiful people make mistakes and become very ugly because of what other people do to hurt you. She said my mom was hurt real bad and never really got over it. Because of that hurt she made a very bad decision because of what happened one day before I was born.

I asked Grandma did she think I was going to grow up and be ugly.

She said, "No baby, you're my handsome boy who will grow up to be a very handsome man one day."

"Well why don't I live with my momma now Grandma?"

"Ervin your mother had a nervous breakdown when you were born. She couldn't handle you and your half-brother, so we stepped in to help her until she could get things together and was able to take care of both of you."

"Is this lady nice like you Grandma?"

"We'll finish this a little later ok. Now you go play upstairs while I fix us some dinner."

I remember overhearing my Grandma telling her best friend what happened that day. She said somebody named Don, who I found out later to be my half-brother, called my Grandparents over to the house and said his mom caught his dad in the room with another man and that my mom was down on the floor screaming to the top of her lungs, "Why Charles why!" Grandma said my mom was on the floor whaling and just kept asking why her, why him, why. Grandma said they both tried to get her up but she just laid there for a long time screaming with tears rolling down her face.

Then all of a sudden mom got up off the floor, wiped her face and walked out the house without a word to anyone. Nobody knew where she went or heard from her for several hours. My Grandparents' took Don to their house and left Mr. Charles in his situation. Mom showed up to my Grandparents' house at 2:30 in the morning banging on the door; she was drunk as shit and said she just wanted to come in for a minute. Grandpa didn't want her to be raising hell in front of the neighbors so he let her in. She smelled like booze and looked like she was half out of her mind.

When she got to the living room she just started laughing and blurting out her drunken story sayin; "I caught that nigga with his lil fuck buddy didn't I. They was havin a good ole' time in there, that is till I popped in onum, haha. Did I tell you what they was doin, let me tell ya. They thought I was still at work but I caught'em. I got off early an came in the house, it was reeeeal quiet. I walked down the hall toward the bedroom and heard Charles saying, "Give it to me just like that," I thought he was in there screwing another woman so I rushed and opened the door and bam, there it was; Charles with his best friend, ass in the air. I was like; dis is a dream right, haha. Let me pinch myself an wake up. I just stood there like a big ass dummie. I shuda ran down stairs, got me a knife and started cutting up me some nigga's. But naw, I just fell on da flo' cryin' like a lil broke bitch. I'll make them pay for this; I'll show'em a real woman."

Grandma said My mom was a mess after that. She felt like she had to prove her womanhood by sleeping with every Tom, Dick and Harry she came in contact with!

As a result of my mom's decision my Grandma told her friend that mom became a whore and that she was the talk of the town. She said that my mom could often be seen taking two or three different men into her apartment at a time; only to have them come out fixing up their clothes. It seemed that I was the product of one of my mom's tricks. How low can you go?

I guess this was true because my Grandma said mom would go over to the base at Fort Jackson on the weekend looking to pick up guys that didn't mind paying for sex. She ended up getting pregnant by some captain over there. They were together for a few months and apparently this captain wanted more of a commitment but my mom was having too much fun opening her legs to as many as she could. Grandma told me she didn't even tell my father he had a son. He had to find out from some of his friends that the chick he was messing with got knocked-up, and word on the street was it was his.

Thinking back, I remember years ago seeing a tall light skin guy in a military uniform come to my Grandparent's house looking for my mom. I remember standing next to my Grandma looking up at his face wondering, 'Who is he?' He searched my face as he talked to my Grandma, I held onto her leg real tight. I remember feeling her tremble just a little bit. She gave him my mom's new address and said, "I don't think you're going to find what you're looking for." The strange man just stood silent for a moment then looked down at me and asked how I was doing. I hid my face in her skirt as I watched him.

When the door shut she told me, "Ervin that was your daddy."

I just stood there frozen. At that time I was about four and a half years old.

Grandma and Grandpa gave me more love than I could ever want. There were times when I heard Grandma arguing on the phone with my mom and things would get heated then they would calm down, and then heat right back up again. One day I found out that all the arguing was about me. My Grandma sat me down at the kitchen table and tried to explain that I was going to go live with my mom and brother. After five years, my mom decided that she wanted to bring me into her home. I thought it was the greatest day of my little life. My mom would finally accept me as her own and welcome me into her arms. Grandma and Grandpa had always been there for me, but now I was about to embark on a whole new fantastic life; or so I thought.

After the news sunk in I was frightened to death to go live with my mom because of all the horror stories that were told to me about her. She talked so sweet and softly, but yet there was something missing. At five years old I could sense that something wasn't right about her.

My Grandma said, "Love your mom and brother because family is family and you can always depend on them."

Mom had her own issues, so; I couldn't figure out why she wanted to bring me into this picture. A few days later my mom showed up to take me to my new home. I was excited about going but sickened because I knew I would miss my Grandparents.

My stepbrother Don and I were as different as night and day. He was darker and much bigger than me. Whenever I saw him he was always grinning like a Cheshire cat. I was skinny, light skin with brown eyes and he was chunky, coca brown with dark brown eyes. He was ten years old when I came to live with them. I remember standing in my mom's house looking around terrified. It didn't look anything like Grandma's place; there was food lying on the table, clothes on the floor and it seemed like everything was out of place. I remember looking up to see my brother gazing down at me with a sly grin on his face. I couldn't tell whether he was happy to see me or if he was going to tie me to a tree and torture me. It turns out I was right about that slick grin on his face. He ended up making me his special project and gave me hell.

I remember how he used to come up to me like he was going to tell me something and then strike like a cobra with his hand and pinch my nipple so hard. It would paralyze me every time; there was nothing I could do but scream. At other times, he would get a wet towel and chase me through the house popping me. I would try my best to hide behind the chair, under the bed, anywhere I could find to get away from him but nothing ever worked.

He would pick on me all the time so I had to quickly learn to protect myself. There were times when I would pick up something and knock the hell out of him when he was watching TV or asleep. My brother was a demon but eventually ended up embracing me and showing me the ropes. He told me he was glad I was there to share his bedroom. It took a moment for me to give in though. I would never let my guard down; it was going to be me or him and sometimes I felt like killing his ass.

My brother would wake up in the morning early and eat up all the cereal and leave the empty box on the counter and empty carton of milk in the refrigerator. I would ask him why he didn't save me some; he would always say, "Every man for himself." Then he would give me that sly ass grin. I was mad as shit cause that meant I had to go hungry until mom came home. Oh yeah, another time mom told us to take a bath cause we both smelled liked mules. Don rushed in the bathroom first and slammed the door. He knew we didn't have a lot of soap, so he would use all the damn soap and leave me with a little sliver; it wasn't even enough to lather up. Again, I was mad as hell.

I paid his ass back though; we both knew mom didn't keep a lot of food in the house but what we had we had to share. Mom went to the store one day and bought some bologna, cheese and some juice. I could see Don calculating how he was going to eat more than me so in my mind I said, "Not this damn time." He was leaving to go to the basketball court, so when mom left the house I went in the kitchen, opened the bologna and cheese, and took all the food out of the original packages. I put half a piece of cheese and a piece of bologna back in the package then I put it in the freezer until it turned brick hard. I took the juice out and poured what I wanted in a separate bottle. Then I filled the juice bottle with a bunch of water and put it back in the fridge. I knew when Don got back from the basketball court he was gonna be famished and head straight to the kitchen.

Sure nuff, when he came home I watched that nigga go to the fridge, get the juice out and put the bottle right up to his mouth. You should've seen his face when he realized it wasn't the regular juice. He spit it out all over the counter and said, "What the fuck is this!"

I sat on the couch with the same shit eatin grin on my face now. I laughed my ass off.

Then he looked at the bologna and cheese, he said, "Ervin, what the hell happened to the food!"

I just looked at him and said, "I don't know, that's all that's left." It was hard as shit.

He said, "I know you didn't eat all the bologna and cheese."

Again I chuckled to myself then picked up my sandwich and started eating. He came over and smacked me in the head. I jumped up swinging like crazy. I knew his ass was hungry but you don't treat your family any kind of way! I ended up with a bloody nose but he had a busted lip. From that day forward he started sharing the food with me. As far as the soap issue, I switched it with some other kind of soap nobody used under the sink. What I learned later on was that was lye soap. You think I ever had another problem with him being ugly about how much soap I got after that? All I can say is that soap tore his ass up.

As it turned out, all the fear I had about coming to live with my mom wasn't about her, it was my crazy ass brother I had to worry about. We began to talk more after that and he told me several times how I was going to see mom bring in men who didn't want anything but sex from her.

I didn't fully understand what he was talking about but it didn't take me long to figure out what he meant.

Because of whatever happened to her long ago, mom was losing herself in any and every man she saw. She didn't want anything from them but a wet ass and a mouth full of cum according to my brother. Keeping it real, mom was fucking everything, sometimes two and three men in the same day. I tried to think of why she was doing it and the only logic I could come up with was that she was so wrapped up in her own self-pity from not having any one to love her. Having someone pretend to love her, if just for that moment, was her only relief. All night long, I would hear creaking of the bed and the sounds of mom moaning and groaning at the top of her lungs. My brother would put his hands over his ears trying hard to drown out all the noises. I was young and really didn't know any better so I just laid in bed trying to figure out what was going on and what exactly it was my mom and that man were doing in her room.

I remember a few times when Don would fall asleep I would sneak out the room and go to mom's door, peak through the hole and listen. I couldn't really see much but the bed would be moving all over the place. With all the moaning and groaning I thought the man in the room was hurting her but she would just keep going and ask for more. One time the door was left cracked and I could see the man down between my mom's legs doin something. At the time it was real strange to me because the man was one way and my mom was the other way with his dick in her mouth going in and out. They never even saw me standing there; I wondered what made them do this. They kept switching positions and doing weird stuff like; the man sticking his finger in my mom's pussy, twirling it around then taking it out and putting it to his nose. He smiled and then stuck his finger in his mouth and put his dick in my mom's pussy. My mom said, "Ride it Mike," as his dick was going in and out fast as shit. Mom started hollering even louder. In my mind, I thought that was just nasty but there were other parts of me that had a mind of its own. As I looked down at myself I noticed my pants sticking straight out cause my little side kick was hard as a rock. I got so embarrassed and ran back to my bed; my heart was pumping fast. I wondered had Don ever seen what I saw and did this ever happen to him.

There was another time I remember that mom had a party. She invited lots of people over and told Don and I to stay in our room. Well, I had to pee really bad, so I slipped out the room unnoticed and mom was in the middle of the room; two men were holding her legs open, and one after another the men were hoping on her like a pack of wild dogs or something. She had one in her mouth and another fucking her. At first, I thought they was hurting her then I heard her laugh. I ran to the bathroom and when I pulled my pants down, there I was again, hard as a rock. I didn't understand how this was happening to me. How was I mad at my mom's behavior with being butt naked in the middle of the living room floor and all these men fucking her left and right, and be excited at the same time? After what seemed like forever, my little water shooter finally went down long enough for me to pee and then I went back in the room. Don asked me had I learned anything. I didn't know what he meant, so I got in bed and just thought mom was really having fun. I wondered did Grandma and Grandpa have fun like that too. It was embarrassing but mom was mom. I learned to love her and accept her promiscuous ways.

Life went on as usual and I got used to seeing the men coming and going. It became a normal part of the day. Even though this was so, my mind hadn't forgotten about the strange occurrences with certain body parts of mine and why I kept getting hard every time I saw my mom fucking everywhere. Something even stranger occured, I noticed a lot of times when I woke up, my little thing was at full attention for no reason. I hadn't seen anything or even dreamed of seeing anything; he was just sticking straight up ready for the world. Even in school, I would get so embarrassed because my dick would get hard for no reason at all. My pants would rub across it a certain way and there he was. I would be in class doing homework or listening to the teacher and out of nowhere, boy yoi yoing. Look everybody, it's the amazing wonder dick! You can't imagine my embarrassment; I had to avoid being called by the teacher and going before the class, keep my hand in my pocket to hold him down while walking down the hallway and God forbid being caught in the lunch line holding my tray and he decided to jump out. I couldn't get home fast enough.

Mom didn't have good housekeeping skills and she hardly ever cooked. There were times my brother and I went hungry all day, and a few times we ate sugar sandwiches with butter and drank sugar water just to have something to eat. I wanted to talk to Grandma but I knew mom would kill me for telling our family business.

One day when I was seven, mom left us all day with nothing to eat. There was boiled peanuts on the stove, so I ate them and the next thing I remember I was in the hospital; I found I was allergic to nuts. I couldn't walk for a week. I missed my Grandparents; I never went hungry or felt unloved with them. There were even times when my brother and I would come home and the lights or water was turned off, but never at the same time; thank goodness.

Mom held a job and several men at the same time. She changed her men as the wind blew and that was often. There was always a different man entertaining her in her room.

As time passed and I got older, I would spend weekends with my Grandparents. There I was shown love and given plenty to eat. I even had a bedroom with my own bathroom in it. I loved taking a bath over there because it was so huge. Grandma would fill the bath with warm water and I would just lay there in perfect peace. I had my first experience in that tub also. It was really strange because again, my dick just stood up for no apparent reason while I was laying there. I looked at it and wondered what was causing this to happen, then I reached up and tried to push it down. I'm not sure what happened but something I did felt kind of good when my hand slid across it as I pushed down. I rubbed my hand across it again and it felt the same. That's when I decided to put my hand around it and move up and down on it. Whatever this was felt great so I kept doing it and that's when this remarkable feeling came over me. I moved a little faster and all of a sudden this white stuff started squirting everywhere and I got scared and jumped. The water splashed onto the floor, my heart was beating fast and I was like, "Woooooooooo, what was that!" I wanted to do it again but when I touched it it was like I was being zapped with an electric charge so I stopped trying and put it off till later.

One of my favorite things of all time was when my Grandparents would take me out to Pizza Kingdom. They would let me eat all the pizza I wanted and after we finished we would go to the ice cream shop. Oh my god that was the best ice cream I ever tasted. I tried my best not to miss a drop but I seemed to have just as much fun getting it all over myself too. There must be something to having a full belly and sleeping cause I never made it back to the house awake. It was almost like a dream because I would wake up the next morning clean like nothing ever happened.

One morning Grandma was cooking breakfast so I came up and stood beside her. She looked at me and said, "Why such a long face Ervin?"

I said, "Grandma, is Don's daddy my daddy?

"No baby."

"Then how did I get here and where is my daddy?"

My Grandma's face looked like I had said something bad; she took a moment before she began to speak.

"Well Ervin as I told you, some time ago your mother had some serious issues before you were born. Because of those issues she sort of went wild and started hanging around in the streets. That's how you got here," she said. "Before your mom got a divorce she began sleeping around with other men and got pregnant with you."

"Do you think my momma loves me?"

"Why yes Ervin, why would you think she doesn't?"

"She's nothing like you Grandma and she's never home. She doesn't even feed us much. She hollers all the time and she always has men coming in and out the damn house."

Grandma's eyes got big and she said, "Watch your mouth boy; things are going to get better just you wait and see."

That same weekend I asked my Grandpa the same question about my daddy. He told me to take a walk with him. We walked to the park and sat down on a bench next to the big water fountain. Grandpa stared off into the sky for a moment and then said, "Ervin your mom has had a tough time and has made some bad decisions in her short life. I can't tell you who your father is or where he is but I'll always be your Grandpa. It might be hard to understand it all right now but you'll learn everything you need to know in time. Your Grandma and I love you very much and think of you as our son so don't worry about where you came from right now. Your mother carried you for nine months but we have raised you from the time you were born."

"Do you think my mom will ever really love me?

He hesitated and said under his breath, "First she has to learn to love herself before she can truly love anyone else." He looked away for a moment then said, "Ervin, don't concern yourself with things like that right now; I'm sure your momma loves you." He took my hand and we headed back to the house. I loved being with my Grandparents.

Then Sunday came and I would start screaming, "I don't want to go back to that hell hole." I hated being there witnessing my mom fucking all those different damn men with her nasty ass. The shit was driving me crazy. I told my Grandparents what I saw and they told me to stop telling people about what goes on in my mom's house. "It's her house and it's her business and you need to stay out of grown folks business." Of course my Grandparents told my mom what I said, and needless to say she wasn't happy at all about me going around telling her business. But I really wasn't telling her business to nobody else except for my Grandparents, and the only reason I told them was because I was hoping somehow they could get her to stop having sex with so many men.

My mom cussed me out and threatened not to allow me to go back over to their house if I didn't know how to keep my mouth shut. She told me that I had no damn right telling anybody about what goes on in her house and if I had that much of a problem with what she does in her own house, I could find me some place else to go. Now if I remember correctly, didn't she come and get me and bring me to this shit hole? I was fine at my Grandparent's house. Anyway.

Being home alone most of the time I decided to start venturing out to see what I could find to play with. There wasn't really much in the neighborhood to do and most of the houses looked sort of messed up. I would spend a lot of time playing in the dirt or throwing rocks at things, or just sitting on the porch watching people come and go. Sometimes I would notice this girl looking at me through the window next door but she never came out so I just acted like I didn't see her. Every once in a while I would see her parents going in or out but they never really said anything either. Strange folks.

One day I saw a small group of guys playing down the street so I walked down a few blocks and just watched them play. The tallest one, Ron, saw me and asked if I wanted to play, and I said yes. He said it was called stick ball and told me how the game was played. The other guys were Michael, Kevin, Steve, David and Tommy. It turns out that Kevin was my cousin but we didn't find out till later. Meeting these guys was probably the best thing that ever happened to me over there. I finally had something to do rather than be stuck in the house by myself all day. I wouldn't stay out with them to long at first because mom didn't want me going too far away.

This again left me with a lot of time by myself to create my own fun. I remember finding some matches one day and making fireballs with some paper in the house. There was something about the fire that captivated me until I held on to a match to long and it burned my finger. I dropped the match and stuck my finger in my mouth quick. Now that the sting was gone another brilliant idea popped in my head. I call this the big fire day, and the day I almost got the beating of my life.

Mr. brilliant idea guy, me, decided to go out back and pile up all the trash, sticks and leaves in a big pile sort of close to the house. I just knew mom was gonna love me for this. Once I finished collecting everything I got my box of matches and set my mountain ablaze. I had to back up cause it got real hot real quick and the flames started climbing. It was beautiful cause all these pieces of floating fires were going all over the place and landing on the grown. What I didn't pay attention to was that they were landing on everything else too. Apparently the girl's dad next door was watching my work from the window and saw that I had put the pile to close to the house. He came flying out the back door and grabbed his water hose and started spraying my mom's house and the fire. If he hadn't done that I would've burnt the house down.

After he finished yelling at me, telling me I was crazy and how I could've killed myself, I told him I was just trying to help my mom by cleaning up the yard for her. He calmed down after that and told me to be more careful, and if I needed help to just let him know before I get started next time. I said thanks to him and he went back in the house. While all this was going on I did notice the little girl and his wife just standing there looking at me like I was the dumbest kid in the world. They never did say anything to my mom and neither did I. She didn't even know it ever took place. Needless to say that ended my fire creating days.

A few days after my big fire episode the little girl finally decided to come out and talked to me. Her name was Crystal and we just sat on the steps and talked about whatever came to mind. She started cracking jokes and laughed at me almost burning up the house. She was really funny and was pleasant to talk to. For some reason I didn't mind talking to her about anything. Whenever we got bored and I was home she would come out and we would just sit on the front porch talking since there was nothing else to do.

A few days later I invited some of the guys from up the street over to the house. We were going to go in and watch TV but Ron and Kevin started looking around with this weird look on their faces. They looked at each other and started grinning. I asked what they were laughing at and they pointed to the wall. I was so embarrassed because I could see some roaches on the wall like they was in a fucking parade; that shit wasn't funny at all. There was food laying on the table from last night, Don had took his shorts off and left them laying on the floor and one of mom's wigs was laying on the floor along with a pair of her dirty underwear. Shit, I knew I should've cleaned up first but I didn't think it mattered much to guys. I told'em to have a seat and each one hit the other like they were daring each other to sit down first. I just shook my head; in the back of my mind I knew they would have something slick to say later. Our house wasn't the cleanest but at least I knew I was clean and my side of the bedroom was clean.

One time I was coming up from the store and I saw three of my friends standing on a old log peeping in my mom's window. They were saying, "Look at that hoe go." I asked them what the hell they were looking at and Kevin said, "Man your momma is a hoe, she's in there sucking Mr. Mike's dick like it's a lollypop." Before I could think I knocked Kevin in his mouth. I wasn't going to let no one call my momma a hoe. I got so angry I was breathing fire. That's when I decided I would never bring anyone in my house again. My mom had no respect for me or anyone else and now everyone knew about her ways. That shit cut deep; I wanted to run away.

But where would I go, I was too young to take care of myself. I became so self-conscious after that and went back to playing by myself. At times I would look up and see the neighbors pointing in my direction; I couldn't say for sure whether they were talking about me but it sure felt like it. I made up in my mind that no matter what, when I got big enough I was leaving this fucking town and if not the town at least I was going to leave my mom's house. She could have this fucked up house and her fucked up life.

Chapter 2

Time went by and me and the guys eventually made up. I was 10 years old now and started running the streets with some of the guys in the neighborhood and chasing after girls. I was really tall for my age; nobody believed it when I told them how old I was so I just started lying about my age. Most of the girls that my brother brought home was around his age or a little older. It seems that if not every day, every other day he was bringing a different girl home. They would go into the room with him and after about 30-45 minutes later, they would both come out smiling with these real satisfied looks on their faces.

One day I deliberately walked in on him; I wanted to know what he was doing. Don was on his knees doing like I seen the man was doing my mom. He screamed at me to shut the damn door; I just stood there for a moment. I couldn't move, what made them do that. I had to know, I wanted to do it more than ever now that I seen my brother doing it too. I would be sitting in the living room watching TV or outside on the steps thinking. I could hardly wait until I was old enough to take a girl into my room and put a smile on her face like that.

At 11, I brought my first girl home not knowing what the hell I was doing, so I invited her to my bedroom. My mom was at work and my brother was at the recreation center. Her name was Tammy, an 11 year old girl that was in my class. I asked her did she want to lay on my bed. She hopped on the bed and I immediately got down between her legs and started to undue her pants. She began to scream and asked what I was doing. I jumped off of her with my mouth wide open, so ashamed. I said, "I was going to put a smile on your face by putting my mouth between your legs." She said, "That's nasty," and moved away from me to fasten her clothes. I apologized and walked her to the front door.

Just as I was opening the door my mom was putting the key in. "Ervin, what the hell are you and this fast tail girl doing in my damn house?" Tammy ran past my mom and down the street as fast as she could go. I told my mom with my chest poked out, "I was doing the same things you be doing when you have men over." My mom stood there and stared at me for a moment. The room was so silent; the only noise I could hear was the sound of my heart beating in my chest. Then in one swift move, she walked over to me and slapped the hell out of me. She hit me so hard I saw stars swirling around as my head hit the floor. She stood over me looking down and barked, "When you think you're man enough to fuck in my house you better be prepared to pay some damn bills and buy some damn food."

I was hoping that she was done, but she wasn't. She walked off and came back with the same look on her face staring down at me for another moment, I hadn't got up yet for fear that she might knock me back down again. "Let me catch you with another bitch in this house calling yourself trying to get some pussy, I'm putting both your asses out." I didn't say nothing, I just laid there until she left the room and then I got up.

That night I lay in my bed, all I could think of was how badly I wanted to get laid; how badly I just wanted to experience it, and how I was going to make it happen. After all, why should my mom and brother be the only ones gettin some? If they could do it I could do it too. I may not know what I'm doing, but I'm damn sure down to learning. I'm gonna get me some booty. (As wonderful as that thought sounded, it would take me 2 years before I got my first piece of ass.)

My next target was Crystal next door; she was two years older than me. I was now 13 and she was 15. It seemed that no matter what else we talked about the subject always ended up on sex. She would tell me how she could hear her mom and daddy having sex and I would tell her about my mom and my brothers' escapades.

We would sit there for hours swapping stories and laughing about it. One day, I got bold and asked her had she ever seen them doing it. She shook her head no, she got quiet then asked me had I ever seen someone doing it? Mr. Macho proudly shook his head yes but I wouldn't tell her who it was. We talked almost every day about sex and doing it. I knew I was going to have her. I just had to figure out how and what I was going to do when the time came. I didn't want Crystal leaving the house screaming like Tammy.

My mom was at one of her spots getting drunk and trying to score her next victim to have sex with, so I knew it would be a minute before she came home. Don was down at the recreation center playing basketball. I decided today was the day I would make my move on Crystal. I made extra sure the house was clean; didn't want the roaches jumping out at her. Her mom and dad was at the pool hall. When Crystal came over to sit on the porch, I invited her into the house; she gladly came in without protest and was grinning: so was I. I got straight to the point. "Crystal we're always talking about sex, do you ever think of actually trying it?"

Before I could say another word Crystal stripped down to her flower panties and bra. She had breast the size of golf balls, not very big but enough to fit in your mouth. I shyly walked over to her and asked her could I put my hands in her panties? She shook her head yes. We both was scared to death. I put my hands in her panties and was surprised to feel all the peach fuzz that she had down there. After fingering her for a minute, I put my fingers to my nose like I seen several of the guys do when they was screwing my mom. It's not like I knew how pussy was supposed to smell, but Crystals smelled a cross between sweet and tangy. She had a different look on her face now, she leaned back and asked me to put my fingers in again. I slipped her panties down, stuck my fingers inside her and started twirling it around; she started moaning softly so I knew it was feeling really good to her. She grabbed my hand pushing my fingers deeper inside, then she looked at me and asked, "Do you want to stick something else inside me?" Afraid that she might change her mind, I hurried up and said yes.

We walked over to the couch kissing as she undressed me. Once we were fully naked Crystal laid down on the couch and pulled me on top of her. Being that I had never been down there before I really didn't know where to stick it. After just laying there on top of her for a minute, I guess she realized that I had no idea what I was doing, so she took my dick and put it inside her. Her pussy was so tight, wet, and warm. This feeling came so quick that I bust before even getting my dick all the way in her. I stopped breathing, my body went stiff and my mouth was wide open; she just kept stroking away.

Let's see, how can I explain this? Thaaaaat shiiiiiit felt grrrrrrreat! Although it didn't take long for my first nut, I stayed in there and matched her every stroke until she came all over me. I couldn't believe how wet everything was. Did all that come from me or her? Did she pee on me or was something broke inside of her? Man I don't know but it certainly did feel good and I was ready to do it again but she said we should wait. Damn!

After we fucked, we cleaned up and got something to eat. For some reason I felt really hungry and full of energy, like I was king of the world. Crystal apparently felt the same because she kept staring at me and smiling. We spent the rest of the day on the porch talking about everything we could think of. As the day came to a close she kissed me and went off into the house. "So wait a minute, is that it?"

Crystal knocked on the door almost every day after that. I knew what she wanted, and it wasn't just to sit on the porch and talk anymore. I was done with her though, I have to admit it was good, but I was on to the next girl. I wanted to be like my brother and find some new booty. I guess I'm just like my brother and mom after all. It was on after that, I started chasing as many skirts as I could.

What slowed me down from chasing the booty was this girl named Jennie, she lived down the block; a little white girl with long blond hair and beautiful big eyes. She was two years older than me and next in line in my hunt for booty. I guess she had been watching me playing with the other guys cause she approached me one day talking about she had a gift for me. I was happy as hell! My first thought was, "Damn she's about to give me the booty and I didn't even have to work for it." She must have saw the lust in my eyes because the next words out of her mouth were, "I don't even know why you're looking like that, because my gift to you ain't my booty." I wasn't even worried, because I knew she was kind of digging me. It was just a matter of time before I got what I wanted, all this meant was I might have to put in a little work after all.

"So Ervin, do you want to know what I have for you?" Hell, since she had already said she wasn't giving up booty, I wasn't really pressed about what she had for me. In my mind at that point there wasn't anything that she could give me better than getting the panties. Jennie told me to close my eyes and open my hand, and when I did she put this little small gold chain in my hand. I was really surprised when I opened my eyes and saw it. I guess by the cheesy smile plastered across my face she already knew that I liked her gift. She smiled, kissed me on my check then she whispered in my ear. "I just might give you some soon." Then she just turned and walked away. As she was walking away, I yelled out thanking her for the chain. Then I put my new gold chain around my neck and walked off thinking, "Yes the booty is mine."

A few days after Jennie gave me the chain, we ran into each other again. She was looking so damn good my dick immediately got hard as hell. I just wanted to fuck her so bad so I could move on. Jennie was alright but I wasn't looking for a relationship, I just wanted to fuck. She asked me where I was going, I told her I was headed to the house. She told me to follow her; I didn't even ask where we were going I just started following her. She took me to some woods that wasn't too far from where we were. I was about to protest and ask her why the hell was she taking me up in some woods, but before I had a chance to say anything she pushed me up against the tree and began to undo my belt buckle.

She dropped my pants, got on her knees and put my dick in her mouth. I couldn't believe it, and I could barely take it. The shit felt so good I got weak in the knees, I started moaning and groaning. I didn't mean to be so loud, but the shit was feeling just way to damn good for my first time experiencing oral sex. I can't really say whether or not Jennie was putting it down or not, because I had nothing to compare it to. But without question she was most definitely doing her thing. She was taking my dick in and out of her mouth, taking it deep down her throat and twirling her tongue up and down. Then she took it out of her mouth and started licking and sucking on my balls.

Now I understood why my brother was always looking so happy when they would come out of his room.

After she got finished playing with my balls she put it back in her mouth and starting sucking it like a lollipop. She was driving me crazy and I was about to explode in her mouth. When I felt myself about to cum I tried to pull my dick out of her mouth, but she grabbed me by my legs and kept on sucking. My knees started getting weak and my entire body started jerking. I came hard down her throat and she drunk it all like she was drinking a glass of cold milk.

After I busted, she stood up, looked at me and started licking her lips, "Damn that was almost better than us actually fucking." Although I still wanted the pussy, I had to agree with her, it was damn near better than us actually fucking. Yes, I admit the shit felt damn good, but I still needed the rush of laying my prey down on the bed and going in for the kill. It was nothing like a good roll in the bed.

A few days later when I went to the bathroom my shit was burning like hell. My dick was on fire and I didn't know who to tell or where the hell to go to get help. I decided to go see my Grandpa and told him what happened with the white girl. My Grandpa shook his head and started laughing at me, and then he had the nerve to start cracking jokes. "Boy you mean to tell me that you're on fire?" I just looked at him because I didn't find nothing funny with my current situation. He took me to the free clinic and I had to get a shot in my ass. That shit really slowed me down. I didn't even know you could get burned from oral sex. I was so embarrassed; I didn't want my brother or mom to find out that I had gotten burnt.

After the trip to the clinic my Grandpa sat me down and lectured me good on how important it is to practice safe sex. Grandpa doesn't even have to worry about that because after experiencing that shit, I was gonna make damn sure I don't ever get that shit again or nothing like it. Dick priority #1! I learned to keep my dick in my pants. I still teased, laughed and joked with the girls but I slowed way down on trying to get up all those skirts.

After that incident I started applying myself more in my studies. I figured that the more I put into my work the less I'd think about girls, and getting some. I ran into Jennie several times after that day. She'd be laughing and grinning up in my face like nothing had even happened. I know damn well that bitch knows she burned me, but she never mentioned it and neither did I. I just wanted to forget it ever happened. Then she made the remark, if I ever wanted some more just let her know and she'd be ready. She doesn't have to ever worry about me doing nothing else with her. Every time she approached me I'd just shake my head and keep on walking.

I felt like putting the bitch on blast, but if I did I'd have to put myself on blast too, and I didn't want anybody knowing that she burnt me. Jennie caught me one day at a bad time, I was already pissed off about something, so when she came with that bullshit, trying to give me some with her nasty ass, I just let her have it; "Bitch what you need to do is go get your damn self-checked and stop going around here burnin nigga's." Her whole demeanor changed, her face turned beet red. I could tell she was mad as hell, but I didn't really care how she felt. She acted like she wanted to say something, but she didn't. She just looked at me, rolled her eyes and walked away.

Life for me at that point was really getting rather boring. I didn't hang out much with friends anymore, and I never invited anyone over to the house. I was always afraid that if I did mom might have one of her trick men over again and I didn't want none of my friends to hear or see her in action; it was bad enough when I was younger they saw her giving Mr. Mike a blow-job.

Arguing with my brother over our mom didn’t help matters either. He would crack jokes and say she ain't nothing but a whore. Even if that were true, he had no right in saying it. We also argued a lot about his dad being gay. In front of his dad he would show the utmost respect to him, but behind his back he would talk about him like a dog. Sometimes Don made me so damn mad I wanted to just poke his fucking eyes out of their sockets. He had a hard time coping with the fact that his dad was gay, but was more troubled by the thought of wondering if it was something that could be passed down from his dad to him and if he was gay or not.

Don would give Mr. Charles hell on some days and get smart by calling him a faggot. One time Mr. Charles heard him and sat both of us down. He explained that just because he liked men didn’t mean that he would love us any less but he wasn’t going to tolerate Don calling him names. He told Don he was old enough to make up his mind whether he wanted to keep building his relationship with him or not. He apologized for hurting our mother but he said some things couldn't be helped. He said maybe one day he would sit us down again and explain some things that happened in his past which lead him down the path he chose. He tried to love our mom but it just didn't work. He told us that we should always give people respect regardless of their lifestyle, then he stood up and hugged both of us. Later that night Don said he would never disrespect his father ever again. I was happy because Don's dad was a good man to me, and he was a damn good father. He always treated me well. Sometimes when he would pick up Don and take him somewhere, he would let me go too.

He was always giving us good advice and showing us tips on how to make money without having a real job. Don's dad tried to act hard core, but he had certain feminine mannerisms that gave him away. He never brought men around us. When we got home after being out with him, the first thing mom would ask us is did he touch us, or had Mr. Charles brought any men around us. One time when we arrived home mom was drunk, she said, "God made Adam and Eve not Adam and Steve." Don would shake his head and walk away. We always told her nothing happened; mom was never going to get past the fact that Mr. Charles liked men. She sat there saying, "Your daddy is a damn fool but I guess you know that right Don." I just sat on the couch listening trying to figure out why she was so mad at us for the way Mr. Charles was. Not that she really cared; she just wanted to argue with him about it. Our answer was always the same "no mom." In the back of my mind I would be saying to myself, he isn't nothing like you.

Don was 19 now and finished high school, and I was in my first year of junior high. Outside of playing basketball and reading comic books I had no real life. I hated being in middle school, it was like a cross from being a kid to turning a teenager. My body and voice had changed a lot. There were a lot more activities and programs in middle school and I was struggling with the fact I couldn't participate in many of them because mom was always either drunk, fucking somebody or supposedly too busy to sign any permission slips, or come to any of the few activities I was in at school. Whenever she would she either showed up late with her titties popping out all over the place and some tight ass jeans saying she forgot or she just wouldn't show up at all.

I invited my Grandparents a few times to see me get awards but I learned not to count on mom. While in junior high I would catch myself daydreaming about what it would truly feel like to know my father. Most of the guys I knew there dad; he may not be all that good but at least they knew who he was. I just had made up dreams of what he was like. If the man I saw when I was five was my father he was light skinned with grey eyes, had broad shoulders and stood every bit of 6'2." I would stare out the window and wish him and I were on the court practicing my skills. I didn't want to play professional ball like all the other guys I just wanted to be good at playing and I wanted to share this experience with my dad. From what I can remember Don's dad didn't play any sports but he did take us to a few games. Now that I'm thinking about it, as young as I was then I even wondered who Mr. Charles was looking at when the cheerleaders came out, he definitely didn't want a woman.

Don struggled with the fact his dad was gay; we talked about why men found other men attractive. When I became aware of the fact that there were differences in men and women and watching women, and seeing people in the act of sexual nature, it always made Minnie Me do things on his own. I had to learn to control my physical emotions while in school because he was just way to free about popping up when he wanted too. The hardest time for me was in Ms. Kelly's class and I believe she knew it. This woman was so fine I really couldn't contain myself. She didn't wear tight clothes like my mom but you could definitely see all the curves in those dresses she always wore. Sometimes I got the thought of pretending to pass out and wait for her to walk over so I could try to look up her dress. And she smelled so wonderful; it was like I was in heaven whenever she walked past. I would close my eyes and try to breathe it all in. Minnie Me was like granite every time and then this soft Angelic voice said, "Ervin are you sleeping in my class again?" I jumped and really did almost pass out. I said, "No Ms. Kelly." She touched the side of my face and said, "Try to stay with me ok Ervin." My heart would beat like crazy and all I could do was just shake my head yes. I'm not sure if she noticed Minnie Me screaming at her but I didn't care one bit.

I also had a crush on big butt Ruth; this girl was so ugly but she had the hottest body with the fattest ass ever. I never let own that I had a secret crush on her though. Everyone picked on her; she had it hard. Me on the other hand, I just blended in; I didn't want others to know I was fantasizing about doing it to girls while in school. I would hear some of the girls saying, "He has beautiful or sexy eyes." I even heard some say I was a nerd. One girl had the nerve to say she heard my momma was a hoe. I wanted to smack her but I remember the words that was told to me, to let people talk; that's what they have mouths for. As long as they didn't put their hands on me or my family I was good so I just kinda looked pissed and walked away. No one had room to judge any one unless they judged themselves first.

Chapter 3

By the time I turned 16 I had a real passion for photography, drawing and film making but my first love was marvel comic books. Whenever time permitted I would lose myself in reading the comic books, they were my favorite. The incredible Hulk was my favorite character and I wanted to be like him, turn my anger into strength and change things in my life for the good. Of course, being able to tear up some shit and get away with it seemed real appealing to me also.

My ninth grade year I did well as far as my grades are concerned. What I had a hard time with was keeping the ladies at bay; it seemed like all of them brought something special to the school year. Brandy was a tall dark skinned girl with huge breastises and a nice smile. I knew she liked me but I couldn't get past her breasts; hell they reminded me of my mom. She made my back hurt just watching her walk by. I did talk to her though, she gave me her notes when I didn't feel like taken my own notes in history class. Then there was Amber, she had almond shaped eyes and a beautiful smile but her body was nothing to write home about. For some reason the room would just light up when she came in; she always smelled clean and fresh. I waited every day for her scent to sashay past me; the scent filled my nostrils and took me places that had nothing to do with school. Then there was my ghetto friend Alisha, she was crazy as hell but I loved talking to her. She was chestnut brown with sandy brown hair and had ass for days; her lil tits were perfect. In my mind all three girls brought something different to me; I could talk to each one of them. I had Brandy for her brains, Amber for great conversation and Alisha for her sassiness and sex appeal; she had great features. It was easy for me to talk to Alisha and she always gave it to me raw; she said whatever came to her mind. Sometimes I would be embarrassed by the things she said but I liked her anyway.

When it came time for the ninth grade prom all three of them asked me to be their date. Hey they didn't wait for the guy to ask them, everyone was scrambling for a date. A part of me wanted to go and another part didn't. I didn't know anything about dancing and I didn't want Minnie Me to show out cause as you can see it don't take much to get him stirred up. If I had to choose I would choose my ghetto friend Alisha; she was the one that brought the most excitement to me. When I was around Amber she stirred me in ways that mentally touched me so she would've been a close second.

What took Brandy out of the running was the fight she got me into. One day I got a hall pass to go to the bathroom and as I walked out the door Brandy was coming out of her class at the same time. She walked over and grabbed my hand and we started walking down the hall. I didn't think anything of it cause this was Brandy. As we walked it seemed like all eyes were on us, then Dean appeared; the biggest nigga on the football team came up to us. When he spotted us Brandy dropped my hand. Dean asked what the hell was going on with the little act. I looked at Brandy and shook my head then proceeded to move forward but Dean moved in front of me. I looked at him sorta puzzled then Brandy stepped in and said, "Dean you know I love you, us holding hands is nothing we're just friends." Dean said that friends don't hold hands and slapped me upside the head. I'm not sure what happened but I think one of the episodes from one of my comic books jumped out and slapped him back. Everyone in the hallway said, "oooooooooooooooooo." Just as he grabbed me and slammed me into the lockers Mr. Shaffer came out and broke it up. I wanted to fuck his ass up but I took the lick and walked away. I never knew Brandy had a boyfriend and why the hell did she grab my hand in the first place? For a moment it felt promising even though I liked her but not like that. I made sure nothing like that ever happened again; I kept my distance from everyone. Alisha and I remained the closest but she told me she would be moving to a new city at the end of the school year. It hurt to hear her say that; I thought when we got to high school I would've asked her out. We hung out a few times after that but I had to guard my feelings because I knew nothing would come beyond our friendship.

When summer came I chose to cut grass to have something to do and a little cash in my pocket. I had a few customers who would allow me to use their mower to do their yard. One particular customer, Mrs. Kitty, wanted me to come by every Saturday at 12 noon; she told me don't be late cause she wanted the yard done before her husband came home. It was an easy $20 bucks, she always had the mower waiting on me. I greeted her and got right to work. One particular day, Mrs. Kitty said she needed some help in her house; I hesitated for a moment then I thought maybe I was going to make some extra cash. I went in and she shut and locked the door behind me. The first thing that came to mind was the movie Psycho cause she started looking at me all weird. She asked had I ever been with a woman and I shook my head no; hell I knew it was a lie but what the fuck. She moved towards me and with one quick step she had my pants down to my ankles. She moved so quick I didn't have time to react. She got on her knees and put my dick in her mouth. I jerked and... tried... to... say nooooooo... please... aaaaaaaah... Mrs. Kitty ran her hand up my stomach and started rubbing my chest. She was doing things I never felt before; I almost passed out. She took my dick out and said, "I'll take care of you," then stuck it right back in.

All kinds of things went through my mind; where was her husband, did she have the nasty man disease? The thoughts quickly went away as I leaned back against the wall and let her work; it had been some time since someone performed this act on me so I lost myself in the moment. My dick felt like a cannon and as my whole body started shaking I erupted all down her throat; the shit felt so damn good. My heart was pounding; when I opened my eyes she was standing in front of me butt naked. I stepped out of my pants as she took my hand and led me to a big couch. She laid back and opened her legs to me; her pussy was smooth as silk. I finally learned how to eat pussy as she gave me all the instructions I needed to put a big smile on her face. My dick was so hard I just knew she was going to let me bust a nutt in her. That's when she asked did I have a condom; you should've seen Minnie Me at that moment. I never seen him go limp so fast and start crying. I was so dumb founded; a condom! This was the closest I had been to a woman in quite some time; I miserably shook my head no. She said this time I'll jack you off, the next time you come bring at least two condoms. This woman was so fine all I could do was shake my head yes.

I put my clothes on, rushed out the house with my towel around my neck and mowed the lawn. The whole time I was going around her yard all I could think of was, "I just had sex with Mrs. Kitty." I'm not even sure I finished cutting the whole yard cause when I snapped out of it I was running down the street. I was hittin that beautiful pussy all summer until the day she said she was pregnant. Aaaaaaa, wa, wa, what! I was like, how she ask me what I was going to do and she made me put two condos on. I'm just going to the 10 grade, a baby. I ran from her house so fast and never cut her grass again. As a matter of fact I didn't cut anybody's yard on that street no more. Hell I was too damn young to be anybody's daddy. I kept thinking, how would I explain that to my Grandparents let alone my crazy ass mom and brother. It was a good experience for my summer though.

Mom told me I needed to find a job during this school year; she said she was tired of supporting my ass but what she didn't realize was you had to have a car to get there. Don works at a warehouse and told me he could probably get me in but he said he may or may not be able to get me there since he would already be at work when I got out of school. I was going into my first year of high school and I was ready for the shit to be over. I could ask my Grandpa to take me to work but I was kinda worried about that once I get the job.

I remember mom and her friend Mr. Mike fighting one night; she asked him to take her to the hospital cause she wasn't feeling well. I overheard her tell him if he gave her anything including a cold she was going to kill his ass. He barked that if she wasn't opening her legs all over town she wouldn't be sick. I just shook my head; being older now I knew what they were talking about. The only worry I had was what did she have; damn was my mom ever going to slow down. Mr. Mike had been mom's regular guy for a long time but one thing was clear; one wasn't enough for her. She still had several dips a week with other men. Mr. Mike and Mr. Charles were the only two that still came to the house unless she brought a stray home, which happened on occasion. I heard mom hollering at me telling me she was going to the hospital and to call my Grandparents if I needed anything. I just shook my head.

It seemed like one minute I was in school and the next I was on break for the holiday. I got a job at the warehouse and things started out working good, then the shit fell apart. Mom started calling the job saying she needed me; she was sick again. I didn't know what she wanted; she didn't want me around her and told me to get a job. Then she gets sick and wants me in the house but doesn't want me to do anything for her. What the hell!

I heard her telling someone she was pregnant but it was in her tubs, and it made her feel like she was dying cause she wanted to fuck but couldn't so when she couldn't fuck she would get drunk as shit and call everybody and cuss them out. That didn't stop her for long cause they had to do an abortion and she went right back to doing the same old thing.

How I got through my junior year was participating in all the school shit they had available. I told mom what I needed to do to graduate; I joined the first computer class ever dealing with learning DOS. We learned the computer inside and out. We had a comic book club and I even joined the Math Team. Hell I did all this shit to stay away from home for as long as I could.

Prom season came around again and I was asked by several girls to go but I had my eyes set on Carmen; she was a hot Latino sistah. She was stacked just right in the back, her hair was almost waist length, she was just the right height, 5' 9," and she had creamy color skin with just a tinge of chocolate in it. Will somebody give me an Amen! Her eyes sparkled to me when she talked; they just captivated me. I asked her on the sly did she have a date for the prom hoping she wouldn't put me on front street by asking so late. But I had to make sure I was going to be able to get a tux, money for pictures and dinner. Everything went as planned until her brother Rico found out I was black. He said there was no way his baby sister was leaving the house with a thug nigga. I was kinda shocked to hear him say that because I was neither of those things. Carmen started crying and speaking in Spanish, but whatever she said didn't work cause he snatched her ass up and threw her over his should and walked off. She went kicking and screaming into the house. I had to admit she was beautiful in her teal colored dress; her hair was in a tight bun with curls cascading down the side of her face and silver eye shadow with dark green and ruby red lip stick on. I just wanted to get close enough to taste that sweet salsa. We were able to take a few pictures together for memories. I ended up going to the prom stag. It was just as well, I needed the money. I had to beg and borrow to get me through another few weeks. My classmates named me Mr. GQ at the prom. I didn't get crowned King because it was my junior year; however I had a few votes. I didn't think people paid me much attention but that night people or should I say my peers were feeling generous. I laughed to myself and accepted the award.

I finally made it to my last year of high school; I was happy as hell! I put all my energy into my class work. It didn't take long before I knew I wanted to pursue development of electronics. I had 12th grade English,

Science, Calculus and entry to computers. I was bringing home decent grades. Since computers were still fairly new I enjoyed getting on the computer learning about the different functions it had and using the phone to dial into other computer systems. I was really intrigued by how the computer worked and its operations. I wanted to know everything I could about DOS and how to build my own computer.

I was basically a loner throughout High school and chose to stay to myself. Other than my friends on the block I didn't really have any other friends. I had people I would socialize with at school but just as school was over I would run and get on the bus. I didn't really want to get to know people because that meant they may want to come over to my house and I sure as hell wasn't going to let that happen. Mom was enough to deal with; I didn't want to get into any fights from someone calling her a whore, even though she was. All my life I was embarrassed by what she did but Don acted like it didn't bother him at all. It didn't look good for mom to have all these men parading in and out of her house.

My electronics teacher, Mr. Guy, told me I was his top student. One day, he asked me to stay after class because he wanted to find out what my plans were after high school. I shrugged my shoulders at first, I had no idea and no one had ever cared enough to ask me about what I wanted to do. Mr. Guy encouraged me to attend college and take electronics as my major. After talking to him, I applied to several different colleges and to my surprise I got accepted to Lyhaven Career Center in Georgia.

Thinking back, high school was a breeze until the last few months of school. I would try and talk with mom about the different colleges I applied to, but she really didn't act like she gave a damn. When I found out that I was accepted into college, the first person I wanted to tell was mom. I guess because even though at times she really didn't act like a mom, if just for a moment, I was hoping she could at least pretend to give a damn and be proud of me.

Of course when I told her, I didn't get that type of reaction, I got the one that I'd been expecting. When I told my mom that I was accepted into college, she asked me was I staying home or going away. As soon as I told her I would be going away, she said, "Good, one less mouth to feed." What the hell!

No "I'm proud of you son" or nothing, but it was all good. Even if she wasn't happy for me I was happy for myself. I couldn't wait until school was over so I could get the hell out of my mom's house, and the hell out of this town period. Don had already moved out and gotten his own place, leaving me stuck here in this whore house with my mom.

I ran errands for my Grandparents and that's how I paid for my class trip, dues, cap and gown. Mom was her usual self; she paid only what she had to, nothing. Every time I told her I needed money she barked, "Money don't grow on trees, get a damn job." I would shake my head, hell I was 18, I could go to work but I had no real transportation and all the good jobs you had to work at night. My Grandparents were a saving grace; they made sure I had all that I needed and more. I stopped talking about mom's exploits long ago; it was all about me and surviving.

Grandpa and I did our usual thing; sitting on the porch sipping ice cold tea and talking while Grandma cooked dinner. I showed my Grandpa the letter saying I had gotten accepted into college. He said he was proud of me and that the difference between me and Don was that I was a go getter, and Don just accepted whatever came his way; he had no drive or personal goals to achieve. That didn't mean he loved him any less he just wished Don wanted more for himself.

Grandma and Grandpa said they couldn't wait for my graduation, and if it was possible they were going to be in the front row. They were looking forward to seeing me walk across the stage and accept my diploma. It made me feel good inside to know they were proud of me. I wished my mom felt the same way.

When Don graduated I remember it like it was yesterday: I just watched as people were hollering for him and screaming his name. There were at least ten different men cheering him on in the audience as he walked across the stage to get his diploma. His dad was the loudest one; without question his dad was very proud of him. Maybe I should've been but I was embarrassed, because some of the men that were at his Graduation were some of the same men that mom had dealings with.

Mom was so happy and excited seeing her son walk across the stage to get his diploma she was jumping up and down like a rabbit, and she damn near broke her ankle. The smile on her face was priceless and I could see the pride in her eyes as she watched him walk across the stage. Don didn't seem to care about none of that, he was just happy to be getting out of school for good. Some of the same men that were at his graduation came over to the house afterwards for the little get together that we had in honor of him graduating. Some of the men even gave him money and other gifts. Don walked around with his chest poked out like he'd done something greater than just graduate from high school. The way he was walking around you'd think he just contributed to saving the world from a nuclear attack. I knew he was just happy as hell, no longer having to be bothered with mom waking him up every morning, nagging him to get his ass up and go to school.

Now that it was my turn, mom didn't seem nearly as interested in me graduating as she was in Don. My Grandparents said they would make sure I got to my graduation on time. On the day of my graduation right before it was time for me to head out, I didn't see my mom anywhere. I knocked on her bedroom door, she didn't answer so I slipped my invitation under the door. My heart was heavy as hell and I knew if she wasn't answering her door there was no way she was coming, but I wasn't about to let her ruin my big day. I arrived at my Grandparents' house and as always I got the love and affection I was hoping to get from my mom; they both made a big fuss over me.

For some reason I decided to call mom one more time just to see if she was coming, even though I already knew in my heart she wasn't. I don't know why I did it; I guess it was just wishful thinking. It was my big day and I wanted her to be proud of me like she was of Don, she never answered. I dropped my head and headed for the car. I fought back tears, because even though I had my Grandparents and I loved them dearly, I wanted my mom to love me; I wanted my mom to be proud of her son on his graduation day. I also thought of my father, and even kinda wished that he could be there. Even though I already knew it wasn't a possibility, the thought still crossed my mind. He probably doesn't give a damn just like my mom. Wow, I'm probably the only kid whose parents don't even want or care about him.

I entered the arena with my Grandparents. I went to show them to their seats before I headed to the front of the auditorium. My Grandpa grabbed my arm and said, "You may be disappointed that your mom ain't here but hold your head up and be proud that you made it to this day and are able to walk across the stage; pick your head up and be proud of yourself."

"Remember son, it's because of you that you made it this far and we're here for you." The tears I tried to fight back came streaming down as I hugged my Grandpa and smiled. My Grandma leaned over and hugged me as well, she said she was so proud of me and whispered in my ear, "Your strength is in God, even in your weakest hour you lean on him. He loves you and his love never fails." I still wished my mom were there, but I felt better. I hurried down the steps, and met my friends and put on my cap and gown. I was ready to do this; finish high school with or without my mom.

The commencement was a breeze. When they called my name I could hear cheers, it wasn't like Don's Graduation but I did get a glimpse of my Grandparents; they were both standing and cheering. I heard a voice say that's my brother. I looked to the left and my big brother Don was there, him and that tramp he calls a girlfriend! He was grinning from ear to ear. I tried to survey the crowd for my mom but I didn't see her. That didn't mean she wasn't there I just didn't see her. I received my diploma and as I was walking off the stage I heard someone say, "Ervin, smile!" Camera flashes were going off and my adrenalin was running high; I was happy as hell to be finished with school. I wondered for just a second though who that was that called my name and took my picture.

After the graduation Don came over and hugged my neck trying to put me in a choke hold, he said, "Let me do this one last time." My Grandparents looked on. Don gave me an envelope and told me to look at it later. I put it in my breast pocket as my Grandparents were gleaming at me with pride. I could see and feel the love they had for me deep down. I was helping my Grandparents up the steps when a voice said, "Ervin Wyatt, congratulations son." I turned to see the man I had seen all those years ago, he was older but still had the same stance and was smiling. I said thank you sir for coming and he said I wouldn't have missed it for the world. My Grandma was clutching her chest saying thank you Jesus. Here's something for you son, take care and then he was gone like a ghost, one minute my father stood before me and now he was gone again. I just stood there numb; I didn't know what to say or how to feel.

Don and my Grandparents stood in the parking lot taking pictures when I heard a voice saying, "Ervin, I'm sorry I missed your graduation but I'm here now." I just looked at my mom; she looked like she was half drunk. I was mad as hell but I wouldn't let her spoil my day, it was a day to be happy and rejoice because I was finished, and I was one step closer to leaving her ass.

A few minutes later Don's father joined us. I was so happy to see him; he hugged me and said he was mighty proud of me. I was just glad to see he had made my graduation. Mom looked at him like she could scratch his eyes out but this wasn't her day it was mine and I was just glad to see one more familiar face! My Grandparents invited everyone back to their place; they had a big feast there waiting. We all ate, laughed and swapped stories about growing up. It was a good evening; at some point mom snuck out but it didn't much matter, I was where I wanted to be, with the people I had grown to love. Don's father handed me an envelope and said, "Son, keep your head up." I thanked him again for coming and he left.

My brother and his tramp left as well. Once I tell you who she is then you'll understand why I call that bitch a tramp. Jennie, yeah the chick that burnt me all those years ago, s he was now my brothers girl and he was so in love with h er. When I first found out about them I couldn't believe they were together. My brother doesn't know about us, I n ever told him and apparently Jennie didn't either. Every time Jennie sees me she gets this sort of nervous, embarras sed look on her face. She doesn't even have nothing to worry about, I haven't told my brother yet and I'm not going to tell him. Not to save her from the embarrassment, but to save my self from it. I didn't want anyone knowing when it happened and I still don't want nobody to know.

At the end of the evening I hugged my Grandparents and thanked them for standing in for mom. My Grandpa said they wouldn't have done it any other way! My Grandma was crying saying there were times she didn't know if I would make it or not. I told Grandma to dry her tears for not only did I make it, but I was also going to college.

Grandpa walked me to the door and stepped outside; he told me to go pick out a used car from one of his friends' car lots and he would take care of the bill. I grabbed my Grandpa and hugged him for which felt like forever, I was so happy. He said please don't tell anyone where you got the car, if they ask just tell them that you got it with your graduation money. My Grandpa said that he didn't want to start a war with my mom or Don, and that's exactl y what it would be if they found out that he bought me a car for graduation, a war.

I was home alone on my graduation evening feeling some sort of way. I sat in the dark, tears spilled from my eyes; I had finished school. My mind drifted back through the day's events. I was happy but sad seeing my father for a few moments and then he was gone. It dawned on me that he'd given me that envelope; I reached in my jacket pocket and pulled out all three envelopes, I didn't know whose was whose now. Don's father left a note, it read, "Today new things will begin and old things will fade away, keep your head up and walk towards your goals." He gave me a $100. The next envelope had no name or anything and had $25 in it. I said to myself this must have come from Don. The last envelope was thicker, I opened it to find several sheets of paper; it was a hand written letter.

Dear Ervin,

Let me first apologize for never being at a game or a program that you participated in. My intentions have always been good. I have lived all over the world never really stopping to smell the roses or plant my roots.

I tried several times to get your mother to allow me to build a relationship with you however she refused. She was instructed by the court to let you come stay with me during the summer months but when it came time your mother would say your Grandparents had taken you on a trip and I would have to plan for another time. Well this went on for years then I just stopped asking her.

I should have pushed the issue after all I have rights to see you and spend time with you, especially since I'd wo n the court order. I just didn't persue it any further, I shoul d have. I paid child support all of these years for a son I hardly knew but I had no doubt in my mind that you were mine, from the first moment I saw you. You were the spitting image of me when I was a boy. I have watched you grow into a man from a distance and I'm so proud of you; I wish you nothing but the best.

I hope this $5,000 will help you get started in whatever it is you have plans to do now that you have graduated from High School. I will always be close by and if you should want or need to speak with me, I will not hesitate to be there for you.

I love you son.

Dad

I unfolded the money and there was $5,000 dollars in $100 bills. I had never seen this much money ever in my life. There was also pictures in a smaller envelope. I saw pictures of me at my sixth birthday party, my sixth grade graduation, my first basketball game, my junior prom and me at school my senior year winning the electronic geek award of the year for having the most potential to go all the way.

Wow he wasn't lying; he has been watching me grow up f rom a far. I cried that night because for the first time in my life I felt rather close to my real dad. I knew that he loved and cared about me. He just wasn't given an opportunity to get to know me. That mother of mine stole my dad from me and she got paid for it. She never let on that my dad was paying her child support. What the hell, I starved and went without clothes, shoes and toys. All the while she was taking the money my father was sending her to support me, and doing God only knows what with it. She damn sure wasn't spending it on me. I could've been living good! She was still my mom but now I was really ready to go to college, if just to get away from her.

Mom always had men coming in and out. I know people had to be wondering whether we had a boarding house for men or something. The men changed daily but sometimes she did keep one for more than a week or two. She had her favorites; Mike was one of her favorites', she saw him at least once a day every week. Then there was Ken, she saw him three times a week. He was loud until he went in her room; whatever she did to him you never heard a peep out him until he came out pulling his clothes straight then he was back to being loud. I would just shake my head. How could my mom keep losing herself in these men? I even wondered whether these guys were paying for sex or was she just fucking to be fucking. That's why I couldn't wait for me to start school; I wanted to get away from mom and her hoeing ways.

Soon I was gonna try and find my dad, he deserves to get to know his son and I deserve to get to know him as well. Mom did her dirt keeping us apart while I was growing up, but I'm grown now, she no longer has that control.

Chapter 4

It was the 80's and you didn't need a lot of money to attend college, but you did need money to get started. I didn't know who to ask for the money, I had already been blessed by my Grandparents with a car; I just couldn't ask them for any more money. The money my father gave me I put in the bank, not breathing a word about the money or the fact that I had seen my father. I couldn't stomach the lies my mom would have told me. She was fighting her own demons. I also knew she wouldn't mention him.

My brother and I talked, he told me to ask his dad for the money to start college. I thought about it for a while and decided to ask him. He seemed to be happy for me and the fact that I had come to ask him and he assured me he would give me the money. I was confident this was going to be the beginning I needed to get away from all the drama that was at my mom's house.

My student counsellor at the college called to remind me that I needed to have my tuition paid for prior to showing up for orientation day on campus. I called Don's dad and left a message and told him that I had until the next day to have my tuition paid so I would be ready for my orientation. I waited and waited, it was the day I was due to Start College; my bags were packed and no step father, no money. I was devastated.

Several months passed and I had no plan in place. I decided to apply to the Midlife Technical College and went to my step father again asking for the money to get me into college. This time he gave me the money.

My first few months in school I took the basic classes I had to have; English Composition I and II, Electrical Circuits I and II, Digital Integrated Circuits, Introduction to Computer Environment and College Trigonometry. I had to have 32 credits to complete my first year so I elected to take Professional Communications and the Approved Social and Behavioral Science Course also. I learned about all of the tech words and their meaning that would help me to get through the computer courses.

I loved going to college; what I didn't like was after class was over I had to go home. Sometimes I'd pull up to the house and there would be two or three cars in the yard. I didn't know what I would find when I opened the door. Sometimes mom would be in her room; I could hear her screaming and moaning as always. She had no shame in her game, she did it and she didn't care who heard her. I was so embarrassed that she would be in the room carrying on like that. I would go in my room and try to study but I couldn't concentrate like I needed; the door banging shut or the doorbell ringing constantly. A few times mom got the nerve to even say, "Ervin if you're home go let my guest in." Since she didn't know I was there I just ignored her and let her let her own damn fuck guest in. I couldn't take it. I wished she would just stop.

I started going to my Grandparent's house to study but even that was a challenge because they always found things for me to do around the house. They didn't understand the concept of me sitting still reading a book or doing research to turn in a paper was homework. The only good thing about going to my Grandparents' house I could eat good. This did give me the extra energy I needed to study and stay on task.

I met some good people while at school, everyone had goals the first year; even though we were freshman everyone had a plan as to what they wanted to do with their degree. I even got to go to a couple of off campus parties; I had a great time. I learned early that I didn't have a high tolerance for drinking but my fellow classmates drank beer like it was water. Then they graduated to hard liquor; I tried to hang with everybody but I knew it was a problem. First, who was going to drive my car and if I got caught drunk my Grandpa was going to kill me. That's when I decided to just be the designated driver when needed and made sure everyone got back safe.

I saw some pretty women while in college too. I thought long and hard about whether I wanted to get involved with anyone. I was still scared I was gonna run into someone like Jennie, and I could still feel the pain of that shot in my ass. The memory that was most on my mind was Mrs. Kitty though; the way she put it on me was like nothing I'd ever experienced before and using the old hand pump was getting old as hell. I decided that if the right one presented herself and the time is right, I would deal with it then. College was a good place to learn how to become self-supportive and prepared me for the real world, meaning a good job so I could support myself.

My classes went well for the first year and a half, but after that, shit started to fall apart at home. I couldn't take the continued stress from everything going on and fell way behind in my work. I couldn't concentrate or focus at all.

My mom continued to have all these different men running in and out of the house. I just lost the motivation to study or go to college, so in order to main'tain halfway decent grades I decided to drop out so I could get my head together. I spent all of the money my dad gave me on gas, clothes and eating good while in college.

When I dropped out I could be found at the library reading or at the movies taken in the newest flick. I even hung out on the corner with my homies; we would drink and be hollering at the ladies. I looked for work and tried to get a job dealing with computers since it was the hottest item off the press. I wanted to stay in the technology field, however, I got shot down because I had no experience.

My first cousin Kevin, my buddy Michael, Ron and me would steal video games then sell them on the street so we could buy beer, wine and gas. Kevin was the one who came up with this bright idea to steal the videos. I didn't really like doing the stealing part but I could sell them like hotcakes. We had a nice little thing goin on and with a little pocket change I was happy just hanging on the corner hollering at the ladies. I wasn't taking them home anymore but I still loved looking at them. Shit, because of my created phobia from Jennie's dirty ass I think I perfected the art of masturbation; I've tried every technique known to man, from the amateur dry run to the banana in the tailpipe trick. Got that one from Playtime Magazine; some guy came up with warming up a banana peel in the oven then workin it out. I thought that was a little weird but it turned out to be quite effective. That Jennie taught me a valuable lesson. Besides that I knew I had to have a job to be able to entertain a real woman; I couldn't even take care of myself at the moment.

Eventually I got tired of hanging out on the block every day with the fellas. Mr. Guy's words still rang in my ears to do something with my life because I was intelligent and could have a good future ahead of me. My next option was to enter into the military. My dad made a career in the service so I was gonna do the same thing. I went down to the recruiting station and talked to Sgt. Thomas about the benefits the Air Force offers and the different jobs that were available to me. He asked me a series of questions about my skills and interests, and then showed me a list of different possible positions to choose from. He said he wouldn't know for sure until I took the ASVAB test because my placement would be based on my score. We talked a little longer and I decided to set a time to take the test the next day.

I arrived at 9am the next day and Sgt. Thomas was there waiting. The test was kind of long but I finished it and passed the test with a score of 83. I was told that I was entering into the delayed enlistment program. That meant I was on a waiting list, so back to the street hanging out with my boys until my turn came up to enter the Air Force.

I almost forgot I signed up for the military because it took so long for them to call me. A few months had past and next thing I knew I got caught stealing them damn video games. I don't know why I decided to change the program but the fella's kept foolin with me and talked me into going in this time to steal 15 videos. I don't know if it was the look on my face or the fact that the backpack I had was making too much noise but just as I was about to walk out the door this big guy stepped right in front of me out of nowhere. First thing came to my mind was Oh shit! He asked me to accompany him to the office; he needed to talk to me about something. The way he said it I wasn't sure if he knew what I had or if he wanted something else. My only thought was, "What's going to happen now?"

Great, now I was charged with shoplifting. Being a great shock to me, my mom went to court with me and told them I was a good kid, and that I was signed up for the delayed entry program for the Air Force. Can you believe that shit? She was actually there and sober at that. The judge said she would expunge my record if I did community service and made restitution for the stolen goods. After completing the community service I went to the Air Force office and explained what happened. I was told I couldn't go in now because I had a record, even if they were expunging it. What the hell else could go wrong in my life?

My life felt like it was spiraling out of control. I only had one more option. I went to the Marine office and signed up, everything was cool until the sergeant came back and barked "Son what type game are you playing!," I failed to say anything about my record. I just wanted to get in the service so I could do better for myself. After explaining what happened, the sergeant told me that they would wave my record. I was ecstatic with the news, I would finally be going into the service.

Mom was happy that I didn't give up on getting into the service, she just told me to give it my best shot. I was going to do more than that I was going to succeed. In an instant she went from being half way pleasant to nothing, like she had just been possessed by something. She was sitting there with this blank stare on her face. I asked her what was wrong; she said your father was in the Marines. Before I could say anything mom got up and left the house slamming the door behind her. What the hell was it with this woman and my father and why was she always making me feel like it was my fault that I was born?

I couldn't stay there any longer so I walked off to clear my head. I started to go to my brother's but he had his own life and place. I hadn't been over there because I still hadn't gotten use to the fact Jennie was his girl. My agenda for the last week at home was to visit my brother and my Grandparents and have some fun since it was my birthday weekend and I was turning 21. It was summer time and hot as hell with a few days left before I was due to be shipped off to boot camp next Monday. I decided to go to the local swimming pool for a dip.

As I walked around the pool looking for a good spot; out of nowhere there she was, standing every bit of 5' 8," coca bronze skin and had a body to die for. Her skin was smooth as silk and she had luscious hips and an ass out of this world. As she spoke I would get caught up just watching her lips move. Yes, she moved me in many ways and mini me was screaming right about now. I know you may be saying looks aren't everything but I wanted her from the first moment I laid eyes on her.

My brain started going crazy and I needed to figure out what my move was gonna be to get her to talk to me without looking foolish. I walked over to her with the straightest face possible and said, "As a courtesy to all our first time guests it is a policy that within the first 5 minutes upon entering the pool area, we give you the option of jumping in on your own or being thrown in. Which do you prefer?"

She said, "I have never heard of that before and I've been coming here for years."

"Oh, then you already know the rules so you don't have a choice, we get to throw you in immediately." I acted like I was going to pick her up and she began screaming saying, "No please don't, my hair." I said, "So you're one of the hair off limits people. Policy says you have to be thrown in twice." I started to pick her up again and she started laughing and backing away from me, throwing towels and cups at me. Everyone was looking at us so I told her that since she had caused such a distraction I would have to postpone the dunking session until further notice.

I introduced myself and told her I was soon to become a Marine and that I would be heading out to boot camp next week. I found out her name was Wynona; she was witty, kind, full of fire and was in school pursuing her degree. I was hoping she hadn't been around with many boys and had the nasty man disease. I was still afraid to pull my dick out. The only way my Johnson came out my shorts was to urinate or when the doctors looked at me when I had my physical to get in the service. Wynona and I talked every day for hours and hours, she was going to the same community college I attended.

She was 20 years old and had a four year old daughter named Angel that she was raising by herself. She shared a small apartment with her mother but it didn't bother me that she had a child as she told me the entire story about how the father left her when she told him she was pregnant. She had plans to get her degree and find a job as a social worker; she wanted to work with people. I just knew I wanted her for my wife.

The weekend came so quick and I knew I was going to be leaving for boot camp soon. I wanted to sample the pussy before I left. Being the king of the mini me special package handling division, my skills were rusty; I didn't even know how to approach Wynona on the subject. She was definitely different, she was a keeper. Time was passing so quickly and I wanted to entertain (make love to) Wynona.

She and I talked all day and all night; she told me her hopes and dreams and I shared my thoughts with her. It felt like I had known her for years. I knew this was a different friendship that was growing and I couldn't help it; I wanted to test that pussy. I hadn't had any in a few years and I was due to release my passion on this bronze sistah. She explained that she still liked to hang out with her girlfriends but nothing would come before me. I told her God and her daughter will always come before me unless we decided to get married. She asked me when I went away would my heart still belong to her. She even asked should we wait to be boyfriend and girlfriend until I came back home. I was like nah, I wanted to make sure she was taken off the market before I left; she said there was no baby daddy's so I didn't feel like there was any competition, just me and her.

I was so embarrassed by my mom I couldn't wait to ship out. I made up my mind that when I came back home I would get my own place. Then mom didn't have to worry about me or my feelings with all these different men parading in and out of her house. I visited Don at his new place; it was an extension of our home; a mess, dirty dishes and clothes everywhere. He was following in her footsteps. I wondered had he learned anything. We had talked about this countless times and we said we never wanted to live like our mom. I just shook my head. That damn Jennie kept looking at me with those big eyes. I guess she was wondering in the back of her mind would I ever tell Don what happened. She watched my every move. I was disappointed cause my brother chose her to be his girl but I vowed to let every man and woman handle their own life for storms would roll in and out. Hopefully by the time I got back from boot camp he will have given her the boot.

After visiting Don I also made up in my mind I wouldn't live like they choose to live either. I wanted my home to be neat and clean. I was wondering, if I could spend my last night before I shipped out with Wynona where would I spend it. I didn't have quite enough money for a hotel stay. I didn't want to go to my mom's house and Don's house was no better but time was passing by quickly. I needed to make a decision.

My next stop was my Grandparents' home. I hadn't seen them much since I found out I was entering the Marines. I wanted to see them before leaving for boot camp. As usual Grandma and Grandpa fussed over me and feed me to death. I had the best meal ever: smothered chicken, rice and gravy, stewed corn, Ice tea, and lemon pound cake. My Grandma was so proud of me. She couldn't help but gush over me.

My Grandpa and I went on the front porch to sit a spell. He asked was I ready to embark on a new career. I proudly told him that this was the best decision I had made in a long time. Then he hesitated and asks had I been putting a helmet on that pipe? We both chuckled lightly; he said going in the service now would take me to some strange places. He said I wouldn't want it (Minnie Me) to fall off while you're away. I shook my head ever so slowly acknowledging his words. I love my Grandpa, he was speaking the truth but I quietly told him I hadn't had sex since I got burnt by that white girl. He raised his eyebrows and said in a low voice, "That's good son but, you will eventually do it again, just protect yourself." I sat up straight with a Kool-Aid smile on my face and said there is this girl I'm interested in and I kind of want to put my stamp on it before I leave. He asked what my problem was, I explained about not wanting to take her to mom's or Don's house; they aren't the cleanest bunch of folk. My Grandpa snickered and told me to wait on the porch. It felt like he was gone forever when he reappeared and handed me a stack of bills. He said, "Ervin, take her to a nice restaurant and then to a hotel, get you some trim. It may not hold you until you see her again but at least the thought will be etched in your brain." I was overjoyed by the love my Grandpa once again showed me, I was so excited. We had a great laugh. Grandpa always had my back.

With one day left until I shipped out, I asked Wynona out on the last night and she reluctantly said yes. I took her to the Little Café on cherry road.

For the first time in my life I felt different about wanting to get the pussy. I wanted to make love to her, and to hold and caress her pretty bronze skin. I wanted to put my mouth in places that were only known by her. The entire time we were at dinner all I could think about was how I wanted to stroke her up and down, plant kisses all over her, leaving my lip prints on her neck. I wanted her badly but it had only been a few days, I wasn't sure whether she would allow me to have her.

As the night progressed we had a great dinner and awesome conversation. My thoughts again drifted to this being my last night to impress her and I know looking at it now that trying to make love to her may not have been the best way, however, I yearn for her. She just made my heart flip when she smiled and the way she looked at me with those almond shaped brown eyes stole my heart. The café we were at had a small intimate dance floor and Lionel Richie's song "My love" came on.

I remember asking her to dance, we swayed to the music and the longer he sang the more connected I felt to her. I looked deep into her eyes as we danced; I gently leaned in and kissed her. It was like heaven had opened up; I felt stars were all around us. She kissed me with such passion. When the song ended I didn't want to let her go. As we walked off the dance floor she was saying, "Now how should we end this special night?" She had this magical look on her face and I didn't want to assume anything but it was as if she wanted me to ask her to spend the night. The bill was paid and we walked from the café hand in hand as we approached the car. I took her in my arms and asked her would she do me the honors of spending my last night with her. She immediately said yes, I stood there a minute not knowing whether to kick my heels or run, I was scared to death!

The night went as smooth as silk. I was in no hurry to rush making love to her, she smelled like lavender. She was so gorgeous in the moon light; her body was perfect, her tender kisses set me ablaze. I gave her the same attention and made sure she was satisfied as well. I enjoyed every moment spent with her. When we got up the next morning and dressed I didn't want to leave her. We ate breakfast and hurried off because I still had to pick up my duffle bag and make it to the airport on time. Wynona and I vowed to talk and write as much as time would allow. As we said our good bye I felt the words "I love you" rolling off my tongue. I meant every word. That's when this little man popped up on my shoulder and said, ("You damn idiot, a few days and one night and you're in love? Really!")

Chapter 5

Boot camp was no walk in the park; I had to get use to someone being in my face hollering and barking orders all the entire time. When we got off the bus we were told to hurry up and get our bags; we were given a list of things that would be expected of us every day. All the drill sergeants were there looking at us. I could hardly contain myself from fear and excitement; I was ready, or so I thought.

The first night in the barracks I heard this loud banging on a trash can and then I heard somebody hollering, "You got 15 minutes to get your asses dressed and down stairs for formation, move it, move, it, move it!." My mind was going 50 miles an hour; I was trying to dress quickly, put my clothes up, make sure my locker and trunk was straight and I had to make the bed perfect in 15 minutes. I had no time to waste; I couldn't look at the others. I made it with one minute to spare. There were a few others who weren't so lucky; Sgt. Gents made them do 50 pushups. He had us standing there in the blazing hot sun for what seemed like hours while he ran down the rules to us.

He said, "The fact that you're standing here tells me that you want to be here. Because you chose to be here tells me that you have gotten rid of your mother and father, which makes me your mother and father now. That means your ass is mine and you'll abide by my rules or you will die. DO YOU UNDERSTAND ME MAGGETS!"

Everyone said, "YES SIR." He turned around and started yelling like a wild man. "Do I look like a sir to you? Do these stripes look like I sit on my ass all day and do nothing but sip tea in the air condition? You will address me as Sgt. Gents, Sgt. First Class Gents or Sergeant, DO YOU GOT THAT MAGGOTS!"

Everyone said, "YES SGT." I thought this man was crazy.

As I stood there I began to say to myself this was going to do one of two things, either make me lose my mind or make me be accountable for my own actions and things to come. Learning the 14 leadership traits helped me see myself in an entirely different light. Those traits were infused in my mind, I thought about them all the time; Dependability, Teamwork, Integrity, Decisiveness, Tact, Cleanliness, Initiative, Endurance, Bearing, Unselfishness, Enthusiasm, Justice, Judgment and Honor.

In our down time, which was hardly ever, the guys were acting crazy saying they couldn't go without pussy. That would be all they talked about in our spare time. I spent my time shining my boots and keeping my locker and trunk straight for I knew the daily inspection was crucial. We had a First Sgt. who just happened to be a Mexican who never smiled. One time when he passed me he slowly walked back, the hair on my neck rose up. I just knew he was going to find something wrong. As always he gave me that smug look but he never sighted me for a violation. Michael was the joker; he had a joke to tell all the time. He would say the First Sgt. was going to catch me slipping one day and I was going to fall in the trap, then he started talking Mexican, as if he was mocking him. I laughed quietly with the other guys. I was known as the quiet one but yet it felt like everyone in my barracks wanted to talk to me. The guys talked about sex but I kept my sex life private because that incident some years ago with Jennie still rang in my mind. My heart was promised to Wynona at home. I yearned for her and I could still smell lavender in my nostrils, it was so sweet to think about. I tried hard to keep her in the back of my mind but that damn Minnie Me just wouldn't stop talking about how he loved swimming in that caramel river.

After settling into the daily routine, I was now learning how to be a Marine. My mind drifted for a few moments to my father, I wondered how he made it. My intent is still to find him and build a relationship with him. I suppose he would be happy that I followed in his footsteps.

There were moments during boot camp that I wanted to pack my shit and run home. That being outside before the crack of dawn, running and exercising was something I had to get used to. And lord knows if it rained it made things that much worse. I had to pass all kinds of tests in the Marines. I had to admit I was worried whether I had the skills to do all the things required to pass. This was still all new to me. Even if I left where would I go? I damn sure didn't want to go home to my mom's house, thinking of that made me work even harder to finish. I didn't care what they might do to me, hell I knew there were better things to come and I wasn't going to give up. I had my Grandparents and my girl waiting at the finish line for me.

The Marines shared discipline tools and helped shape me to become part of an elite brotherhood. They enabled me with leadership traits that I could use with honor on and off the battlefield. I knew I was born to be a leader. I was going into weapons operations after graduating from boot camp.

After an amazing 12 weeks it was my graduation day. I asked my mom, brother, and Grandparents to come out to see the transformation. I have a purpose and this moment is the defining point in my life where I will lead, honor and support my country. I have been trained to act instinctively and effectively. Looking at the thousands of people that were in the audience I searched for my family, not showing any emotion. I saw that it was only my Grandparents. I was so proud to stand before them as a Marine, I never asked why my brother and mom didn't come I just enjoyed the moment of seeing my Grandparents. I could tell they were very proud of me. At one point I wished Wynona had been there, she supported me the entire 12 weeks never whining or being insensitive to my goals and the process in which it took to get to this special day.

I spent two days with my Grandparents. Grandma was so proud and kept saying she knew I could do it. Grandpa and I spent some time alone; he asked, "Did you learn anything about fighting for your country?" I said, "Grandpa, the skills I learned about leadership and serving my country were an eye opener and a privilege to become part of an elite brotherhood." He knew about those leadership traits. He shared some of his experiences as a Marine. I listened patiently. My heart was full of emotion, Grandpa was beaming with pride and I was now ready to find me a good job and prepare for my future.

My Grandparents flew home the day before I was to return to civilian life. They said they would see me after I had gotten home. I would still have to report one weekend out of the month but I looked forward to seeing my brothers.

When I arrived at the airport Wynona was there waiting on me, I was so excited to see her. It seemed as if her cocoa bronze skin shined so bright I could hardly contain myself. I don't think I need to mention that Minnie Me was already at attention right. That is, of course, until I say the other surprise at the airport, I met Wynona's daughter Angel for the first time, she was just as pretty as her mom. We kissed and embraced, it seemed like forever. I even got choked up thinking this was going to be my little family! Wynona and I talked all the way home and made plans to get together later. I had to at least go home so my mom could see me in my uniform.

After coming home from boot camp things with the family had somewhat changed. My brother was expecting his first child with that tramp Jennie, I just shook my head. Mom was still mom bringing tricks home two and three times a day. All she cared about was that wet ass. She seemed excited to see me but gave no explanation as to why she didn't fly out for my graduation. I showed no emotion for this was the second most important time in my life. I had asked her to come and support me only to be let down again. I vowed I'd never ask her to support me ever again.

My mindset had changed, God knew it and so did I! I set goals for myself while in boot camp. Look for a place to stay, find a job, date Wynona and prepare for the future.

My thought process was to change my living arrangements immediately when I returned home. I looked for a job and as I did that Wynona and I became very close. We spent every moment we could together; she even went with me to find an apartment. It was a cute two bedroom that I could afford. I was so glad I didn't have to return to my mom's house for a long period of time. Her life hadn't changed one bit in those 12 weeks, things were still the same.

I bought the necessary things I needed to move in and would gradually upgrade and buy additional things as I could afford it. My Grandparents were again a saving grace, they gave me all of the household things I needed for my bed and bathroom. I was fine with just having the four walls and a bed. Anything would beat coming home and hearing my mom laughing and that damn bed creaking.

That thought in mind, I was about to make my own bed creak. The difference was I'm in love with one woman. Marriage was in the plans but I wanted to wait awhile, there was no need in rushing because I had her and she had me.

The first night in the apartment Wynona and I spent alone; we made love most of the night before drifting off to sleep. The next morning I asked her what she thought about getting Angel and moving in with me. I remember the look on her face like she didn't want to do that. I wanted to be a family man and I wasn't going to leave her child at her grandmother's house when we could take care of her, at least on the weekend.

I spent most of my days looking for work; it was just a matter of time before I found the right job, I had to remain patient.

Chapter 6

Through my travels I'd see familiar faces and one particular day I ran into Crystal. It had been several years since I had seen her. We chatted for several minutes catching up. I felt bad because all the memories of what I did to her came flooding back. I was embarrassed now by my behavior back then. Crystal was beautiful, she was soft spoken and a joy to speak with. She said she was being guided by God to finish her education and live a life that God would be pleased with. I had a big grin on my face and I was happy to hear she was doing extremely well for herself. However, I knew nothing would ever become of this conversation because my heart belonged to Wynona. Crystal and I exchanged numbers, hugged and said our goodbyes. The moment we hugged something very strange went through me. I couldn't shake the feeling.

When I arrived home Crystal once again faded from my brain as Wynona stood before me. Something shook me to my core, I didn't want to hurt another woman by making love to her and not being man enough to step up to the plate and marry her. I thought back to several conversations my Grandparents had about people living together in sin, it weighed heavy on my heart for some reason after seeing Crystal. I no longer wanted to wait to get married; I wanted to get married as soon as possible. My Grandparents had instilled some family values in my head. I knew I didn't want to be like my mom or my brother. Don was having his first child and he wasn't married and my mom was on some other shit. Do as I want to do, fuck who I want to fuck. She didn't care what anyone thought of her or her promiscuous ways!

A month passed and I had a plan in place, I bought a ring and proposed the next week. Wynona was so happy and so was her mother. I didn't discuss it prior to doing it with my Grandparents or my mom, it was my life and I was grown. I felt they would be happy to hear I wasn't just sleeping around. I was being my own man.

We went to the Justice of Peace on Wednesday afternoon. Her mother and our daughter were there. As soon as we said I do Wynona said she was going to go meet some of her friends and share the good news. I had a plan as well; I wanted to take my wife and daughter to dinner. She said we had plenty of time to do that. She seemed so excited to go tell her friends she was married. I reluctantly said, "Go ahead, I'll watch our daughter." The day was still young; we could consummate our marriage later that evening.

Oddly enough Angel and I stopped by my Grandparents' house. I shared my good news that I had gotten married. They both stood there with puzzled looks on their faces. Then my Grandpa spoke up, "I'm glad for you son but where is your bride?" I chuckled lightly, "She went to go share her good news with her friends." I saw Grandma's eyebrows raise; she threw up her hands and waved them in the air walking away saying, "These young people have no idea what the hell they're doing." I stayed a couple of hours talking and of course it wouldn't be my Grandma if she didn't feed me. She took Angel and went in the next room. My Grandpa took me by the arm and led me outside. He said, "Are you sure you made the right decision, you hardly know this girl." I shook my head yes, I was adamant in letting him know this was one of the best decisions I had made. My Grandpa said normal couples don't start their first day of marriage not together, they cling to one another.

I assured Grandpa that my wife was a good woman; she just wanted to share her excitement with her friends. He said, "Well hell, you should've gone with her, you're the show piece. Instead you got her daughter and she's nowhere to be found, sounds a little familiar to me." I shook my head, "No Grandpa I chose to keep my daughter while she goes out." My Grandpa shrugged his shoulders, he looked disappointed and I knew if he was, my Grandma was to. What they failed to realize is it's my life; Maybe I could've made her go out with me instead of going over her girls house. That's when that little guy popped up again and said, ("Pussy whipped after two nights and dissin' your Grandparents already, you da man, dummy.")

I went home only to find it empty. I knew this marriage was of two young people coming together because they loved one another, I didn't want to be a control freak. I found it very liberating to let my woman go and do her thing. At the end of the day I knew she would be coming home to me.

Crystal happened to call later that evening as I was waiting for her to return. Without thinking I blurted out, "Crystal, I got married today!" I can still remember the strange silence between us on the phone that day. She gave her congratulations. I told her that we could still be friends because we all needed friends. ("Damn dummy!")

I went on with my life and attended drill. Two weeks after I got married I landed a good job with a nuclear plant.

Everything seemed to be falling into place. Wynona and I were good for each other; we helped one another with everything. She asked for advice on her work in college and I was glad to help her. She helped me prepare for drill once a month. It seemed as if our little family was the greatest ever. Our love life was so loving and compassionate. She stirred something in me; I craved her morning, noon or night. I was so in love and wanted her so much that I had to keep my hand in my pocket most of the time just to keep you know who hidden from spectators while we were out. Was I really that out of control? This can't be something that anyone else has experienced before. I got to calm down.

At some point I got around to telling mom I was married and the only thing she said was watch out for a woman who doesn't like her own child, she has secrets. The words, "Sounds like someone else I know. Must take one to know one," came so quick and as the first word jumped out my mouth I grabbed a bottled water and drank it down. I played it off and shook my head; I knew my mom knew of Wynona but to what degree I didn't know. Why would she make such a statement? This brought back some ugly memories for me as to how she was when I was growing up.

I was doing whatever I had to do to take care of my family. One particular time when I left for drill, upon my return home I ran into a few of my buddies. They told me they saw Wynona at the club shaking her ass on the dance floor like she wasn't married. I didn't get mad, I simply talked to her about what I heard. She started yelling and said I was reading too much into what my friends were saying and that everything was good. ("Get ready mister man. Numb nuts!" Does anybody else hear this guy talking?)

It saddened me to think that my wife would be in a bar when I was away. It scared me to think about it because it made me think about my own mom and how she carried on in bars. Could this be the beginning of a serious problem? I said to myself "You need to stop, that's your wife stupid."

I prayed for guidance, I wanted nothing but the best for my family. It seems like when I was depressed or feeling low, Crystal would call. She always had encouraging words to say and she said she was being lead to check on me. I found this refreshing and thoughtful. Her and I would talk, laugh and then she was gone again. That same feeling always came flooding back after each conversation.

Wynona would act as if she didn't want to be married at times or have children and became very jealous of the fact I had myself together. I had a plan to build a comfortable life for me and my family. Instead of assuming the worst I decided to work on my marriage. I hoped that what I was feeling would go away and in time she would grow to love me, and the few differences we had would fade away.

Chapter 7

Working as a nuclear plant operator Monday through Friday was alright but it was starting to get a little boring. All I did every day was adjust controls to generate specified electrical power and regulate the flow of power between generating stations and substations. Hell, the plant basically ran itself, I was just there to monitor. To have a change of pace I decided to pick up a third job as a correctional officer on weekends. I thought this job would be kind of fun but boy was I wrong about that.

The only fun thing was Kevin worked there. I hadn't seen him since we had the run in with the law; his record had been expunged too. Although we work together we worked on different tiers; I was responsible for tiers 2 and 3 and he worked on 1 and 4. We started meeting for lunch at the same time. The guys on the job would shoot the breeze, talk about their families and doing extra activities after work to take the edge off. I would just listen; I didn't want to expose my family to work life.

Kevin would talk about his private life; he even shared a few stories about his wife and new baby boy. All of us were young so working two jobs was good but it added more stress. The first week I started working one of the inmates threw feces on Kevin. The other guards beat the guy down like he was a dog or something. I felt so bad for him but Kevin said it came with the territory. I made it my business to call home every night to let my princess know I loved her. Sometimes she would answer wide awake and other times I would catch her sleeping. I loved my wife and was willing to do whatever it took to make her happy!

Working as a correctional officer was much different than sitting behind a monitor. I heard a lot of things and I saw a lot; I just had to pick and choose whether I would approach an inmate for something I saw or let it go, I was still considered a rookie. I didn't want to see any of the inmates get beat like the other guy over something that could have been handled totally differently.

Working 7 days a week left no real time to spend with my Grandparents or visit my family. Mom and I would chat on occasion over the phone. Don and I did the same thing; we would catch each other when we could. I guess I didn't really think things through before I jumped out there but it's all good.

Don and Jennie were expecting a little girl any day now. I even wanted to go back to school. I was willing to do anything to keep my family comfortable but yet there was a deep dark feeling growing within me that it was still not good enough for the love of my life.

Don's daughter Briana Renee Parker came in weighing a whopping 10 pounds. My brother was so happy he was a dad and begged me to come to the hospital to meet my new niece. Against my better judgment I prepared to go meet her. After about an hour Wynona and I went to give our congratulations. Entering the room it was quiet at first as the four of us never really spent any time together. Jenny was lying in bed with the baby up on her chest. Briana looked like a little white ghost. Don kept encouraging me to hold my niece. Jenny and I looked at each other, she hesitated for a moment, and then she gave me the bundle of joy. I took a seat and looked at this precious child, she was so beautiful. I looked at Wynona to see her expression; No sign of a smile, she just had this blank look on her face. Don said, "Wynona I guess you'll be next, you gonna give my brother a son?" Don laughed all hard, Wynona looked away and didn't find what he said amusing; she hardly even looked at lil Briana. I said,

"Thank you lord for this bundle of joy." I thought this could have been my seed but thank god it wasn't. Don was a father.

At that moment my Grandparents came through the door. Grandma said let me see my first great grand. I handed the baby to her and kissed her on the cheek. She asked how I was doing. I told her I was doing well. Grandpa looked at Wynona, he said, "How are you doing young lady you taken care of my grandson?" Wynona drew closer to me and nodded her head, "Yes sir we're doing fine." I put my arm around her, she made me proud ("Here we go again dumb ass trying to make it more than what it is.") Grandma said Briana was going to be a beautiful mulatto girl. Don stood with his chest poked out, "Nah, she African America Grandma." Grandpa chimed in, "Son we know she African America, your grandmother is just saying she going to be light bright." Jenny turned beet red. We all laughed and enjoyed the new life that had been added to our family.

Mom showed up late as hell, as always. On that note that was my queue to leave. Wynona hardly spoke to my mom; she looked at her as if she had seen a ghost. On the way out she was awfully quiet, she said she didn't like hospitals or new babies. I asked her why she felt like that. "She said, "I guess because they don't really have any personality and they're solely dependent upon their parents." I grabbed her hand and kissed it. I said, "That's how their little lives are supposed to be, depended upon the two people who love them the most." On the way home I was troubled that she felt the way she did. I wondered why she felt like that because when she had Angel she was alone, no baby daddy in the picture.

Wynona got pregnant a year after getting married. She wasn't happy about being pregnant. I explained that this would fade away once the baby arrived. I felt I needed to do something to pick her spirits up. I secretly started to look for a house. I didn't want to bring my baby into a two bedroom apartment that didn't have a washer, dryer or room for my children to grow. After a few weeks I found the perfect home. It had four bedrooms, two bathrooms, a huge great room, nice kitchen and plenty of back yard for the children to eventually run around in. I knew I had less than three months to get us moved. I was told I could close on the house in 45 days, so that left me a little over a month to plan the move. I wanted so badly to please Wynona. I went to my Grandparents and enlisted their advice and help. They had eventually calmed down from the news of me marring Wynona and I wanted to share my excitement and needed their help. I was going to buy the house and plan a baby shower for my wife along with a house warming party. I just knew this would make her happy. ("If I was just a little bit bigger I would slap the shit out of this fool.") Wynona was always complaining she didn't have as much as her friends had. I explained to her that I had to wait until I could establish some credit and then we would upgrade our living quarters and car a little at a time.

Everything was in place for us to move. I held this secret long enough and I planned everything out; the keys to my new home were in my hand. I worked in the house for a week a few hours at a time getting everything ready. I just hoped Wynona was going to like what I had done. I picked out the colors for the rooms, bought new furniture so the only thing Wynona would need to do is decorate the babies' nursery. ("You big dummy, what woman do you know that doesn't want to have a say in how her new house is to look? You da man big daddy you da man! For the record everybody, I tried to tell his ass.") I invited a few friends and family to meet me at the new address because it was a surprise to Wynona. I wanted to be the one to bring her to our new home. My Grandparents had picked up our oldest daughter Angel. Wynona's mother was even going to be surprised along with my mom.

Wynona seemed like she was getting too big to quickly for her to be just five and a half months along, and she was very cranky. I told her I wanted to take her on a date; she said she didn't feel much like going out. I laid a dress out and told her to get dressed and that she would feel better once we were out. She moved like a snail but reluctantly she got dressed. I looked at her and smiled, her belly was so beautiful to look at; she was a flower blooming for all the world to see. I had to catch myself, didn't want my emotion to get the best of me.

Wynona got in the car fussing saying "We could've just stayed home and watched TV."

I chuckled a little and said, "No baby, this is a very special day, you need to get out and get some air."

She asked, "What makes this day so damn special, it's just another Saturday to me." I reminded myself that it's just her hormones kicking in. I had been doing a lot of reading about babies, pregnancies and women, and what they go through while carrying a child. It was a lot to absorb but I was definitely up for the challenge. This was my seed she was carrying. I made a vow to God that I would never leave my child and I would always be there to protect, teach and love him or her.

We were riding along; I told her I wanted to stop at one of my home boys' new house for a few minutes if she didn't mind. She wrinkled her forehead and asked why we had to stop over there right now; she wasn't in the mood for visiting folks. I calmly said, "Will you please just do this for me." I leaned over and planted a kiss on her soft lips, she rolled her eyes and her face came to life. We both got out of the car; there were several cars in the drive way but none she recognized. I took her hand as we were walking up to the house; she stopped and said, "I love their front yard it's beautiful."

I clutched her hand even tighter and said, "So you like this huh?"

"Oh yes, maybe one day we can have a house like this, and a yard with shrubs and flowers."

I said, "It's coming, just be patient babe I have a plan."

She smiled and giggled. The plan was I was going to ring the doorbell and once someone opened the door I was going to let her enter first and everyone was going to say surprise. My heart rate was going through the roof; so far so good you never know with Wynona what she would do next. I rang the doorbell and guided her in front of me. I kissed her neck and breathed in the scent of lavender which always soothed me and the door opened. She walked in first and as soon as I walked up behind her everyone said surprise, welcome home!

She stood there in utter shock. She turned around and looked at me with the most innocent look ever. She asked, "What they mean surprise Ervin." I took her hand and walked her into our formal living room where a banner hung; it said welcome home to our first home babe!

As she stood there trembling a few of her friends came out of the shadows and grabbed her saying, "Girl come look and see what your husband did all by himself." She looked at me and I could see joy in her face, I blew her a kiss and she was gone. The doorbell rang. I went to the door to open it and there stood our oldest daughter with my Grandparents in tow. She grabbed me saying, "Hi daddy, where is mommy? I missed you and her." I picked her up and nuzzled my nose in her neck and told her welcome home sweet heart. She started squirming so I let her down.

Wynona appeared again with this huge smile on her face. She greeted my Grandparents and stood with me. I finally felt loved at that moment, she looked pleased. Family and friends came and went, my mom even showed up bringing her favorite boiled peanuts. I just laughed to myself. Don, Jenny, and Briana were one of the last to leave. The year had gone by so fast. Don and Jenny were still together; their daughter was so beautiful but she had yet to mumble her first word. As quiet as it was kept, I learned that Brianna was going to be deaf. Only time would tell how things would end up for my niece. I thought several times maybe this child had been marked in some way because of her mothers' ungodly deeds. I still loved my niece any way. In a few months I would be having my first born. Angel would always be my daughter; however, having your own seed is something special. Today we all seemed to have gotten along for once.

I slipped away and stood on the back deck alone. I thanked God for helping me to do all of this so I could make my wife happy and give my budding family a safe place to live. As I stood there with a glass of wine in my hand, again I thought of my father for a few moments. I made up in my mind when the dust settles here and before the baby arrives I was going to try and locate him.

Chapter 8

The first night in our home Wynona allowed me to make love to her, which was rare since she was pregnant. We started out just kissing and fondling, she loves the feel of my fingertips running along her soft velvety skin and I love seeing her reaction as I find each secret spot. As I continued to stroke her lovely body my lips went to her breast, I licked and sucked her nipples until they were firm against my tongue. I worked my way down to her swollen belly and kissed her ever so gently. I could feel the fire mounting inside me or maybe that was just Minnie Me pocking me in the stomach. He's always so fast but he had to wait.

She didn't ask me to stop; she arched her back as if she wanted me to continue. I kissed and licked until I found her most intimate place. I could hear her moan each time I gently ran my fingers over her sweet little clit. As I licked and nibbled more I could feel her clit become harder and I knew she would have an orgasm soon. I wanted to milk this pleasure for as long as I could so I slowly circled her clit with my tongue, taking the tip and brushing it with my tongue faster, then slow and fast again until I found myself in a rhythm that felt like she would explode any moment. She moaned and whispered please don't stop. To increase her mounting pleasure I slid two fingers just inside her flowing river and slowly began to rub her G spot as I sucked the head of her clit until I could feel the juices on my lips. I don't know about you but the hotter she got the more excited I got cause my little man was hard as steel.

As she was beginning to reach the peak of her climax I slowly laid on the side with her in front of me, raised her leg and gently entered from the back. Her silky wet pussy felt so good as I went deep inside her. She knew how to draw me into that pussy; she had a way of working those muscles as she rode my dick gliding in and out while I kept stroking her clit with my fingers. As she began to melt she tightened her lips around my dick and milked me for everything I had. I didn't want to climax but it had been some time since I felt her pussy around me and I came like never before. I wanted to stay inside her for as long as I could cause I didn't know when the next time she would allow me such pleasure. I loved making love to her, she took me places I had never been and she consumed my mind, body and soul. She made my entire body shiver from her love. Our first night came to a beautiful close as I lay there and drifted off to sleep watching my princess in perfect peace.

After being in our new home a short time Wynona and I got into a big fight. She was nearing her due date. I asked her not to go anywhere without me just in case she went into labor. She said I was smothering her and she needed room to do her. I detected anger, I knew she was uncomfortable but I had no idea she felt the way she did. For the most part I tried to reason with her, letting her have some space. Any day I was going to be a father and I was excited. I just wanted to make sure everything went the way it was supposed to. Reluctantly I dropped her over her friend girl's house; she said she would call when she was ready to come home.

Sitting in the house with nothing to do I sat there thinking I wanted to find my father? I searched for my birth certificate; I remember years ago I saw a name on it but I wasn't sure of what it was. I got my brief case and retrieved my birth certificate. Looking at the document, my hands trembled, Ernest Wyatt is my father. I wondered was he my dad or just a name she placed on the document. Right now I knew he was a high ranking official. I got on the phone and called the Marine office, I knew a few people on the inside. Molly was a ditzy blonde, I knew her from boot camp; she ended up working in the local recruiting office. I asked did she have an Ernest Wyatt listed as an officer in the service. I explained that I just need to know whether the name came up. She said give her an hour.

I paced the floor thinking of my father, the arrival of my baby, Wynona and just life itself. The phone rang, Molly said, "Ervin we have several Ernest Wyatt's but there is only one African American Ernest Wyatt in this region. Why do you need to know?"

I hesitated a moment, "He may be my father."

"I'll tell you this and then I'm gone! He's been in the service longer than you have been alive, he retires next year."

"Molly, one more question please, this is so important. Is there a picture there of him?"

"Ervin I can't, I could be fired for this."

"Please I need to know, I know you've seen the picture do we look alike."

"Ervin I can't." The phone went dead. I slammed the phone down! Like everything else in my life I still didn't feel complete. I needed to know whether this man was my father. The phone rang again; I snatched it up saying hello.

"Ervin can you come pick me up, I'm ready?"

"Yes baby, I'm on my way." Getting in the car and driving, past images flashed in front of me. I was a boy again; I could see the man my Grandma said was my father. I could also see my graduation day and the man that stood before me. I did look like him but was he really my biological father.

I picked Wynona up and she seemed happier than when she left. She wanted to go get something to eat. I suggested that we go pick up Angel first and then we could all go grab a bit to eat. Wynona became infuriated by this and I asked her why she always caught an attitude when I ask about our daughter or included her in our plans. It was bad enough Angel was always with Wynona's mom. I didn't like it one bit. Wynona said, "You're not her father why do you care. I pulled the car over gripping the steering wheel and biting my tongue, "When you asked me to be in your life I accepted Angel as my own. I may not be her biological father but I'm the closet thing she has to a dad." ("Whup her ass nigga!" What!) I will not allow you to continue to treat her differently. She said, "I can treat my child anyway I like, who the hell are you to tell me how to treat my daughter." ("I said whup her ass nigga!" Will you please shut up!)

"Wynona, before I say something I don't want to, let's get something straight. Angel spends way too much time at your moms, she belongs with us. The reason Angel cries now when I go to work is because she doesn't know when she will see me again because you always tell your mother to come get her."

"Ervin I can do whatever the hell I want with Angel and there isn't a damn thing you can say about it."

"Wynona, I'm telling you if you don't stop you're going to pay for it later, trust me. Angel needs to be with us point blank, her sister or brother will be here any day and I don't want them to be separated for no reason."

Wynona screamed to the top of her lungs, "Take me home damn it, right now! I don't give a damn what you do just take me to the house."

My next words were, "No, get yo evil ass out of my car and walk. I don't care who may have done what to you, Angel is an innocent child and doesn't deserve to be treated like something lower than an animal." I opened the door from the inside and told her to get out.

I started the car and headed towards the house mad as hell. I was in fuck Wynona mode. ("It's about time you came to your senzes." Man shut up, you can't even talk right. "At least I know when to whup a chick ass." Wateva!) I was going to get Angel; if I don't put my foot down Wynona will think she's running the house. To blow off some steam I drove around for a few minutes and it ended up taking me 25 minutes to reach Wynona's mother's apartment because I had to cool off a little first. As I stopped the car a taxi pulled up behind me and Wynona jumped out slamming the door. She walked past and went into the apartment. I waited a few minutes, no Wynona. I tapped my fingers on the steering wheel trying to calm myself down again. Still no one came out.

I took the keys out the ignition and headed toward the apartment. I knocked on the door, no one answered. I knocked again, Mrs. Cary answered the door. "Hey Ervin come on in, how are you today?"

"I'm fine Mrs. Cary is Angel and Wynona ready?"

"Ready for what Ervin?"

"Well I told Wynona that we needed to come get Angel because she belongs with us, not here with you all the time. You need your space. She just came up a few minutes ago."

Mrs. Cary looked mystified, "What are you talking about Ervin, I haven't kept Angel in months. She's been round her daddy house most of the time. Wynona or Mike might bring her by and say hi but she don't be here son, and Wynona's not here either." ("Suppa nigga, it's ass kickin time!") As good as that thought sounded I forced myself to keep cool.

Mrs. Cary looked up at me and said, "I be damn, Wynona got you thinking she be here with me." She shook her head in amazement, "I told that damn girl some time ago to tell you that she was seeing her daddy and that you had a right to know."

I calmly asked, "Can you tell me where he lives?" Mrs. Cary stood there for a few moments not knowing what to say or do and then there was a knock at her door, then keys rattling. She said, "That must be Wynona right there." I just realized that Wynona hadn't been in the room the whole time we were talking. I stood straight up as tall as I could and wondered how the hell was she going to fix this damn lie up.

Struggling to keep from putting my hands on her, she just stood there in the living room with this stupid look on her face. Angel jumped up in my arms, "Daddy I missed you"! Fighting back tears of anger, I hugged her and told her how I missed her too. I put her down because she smelled like men's cologne. The smell only fueled deeper thoughts and I had to calm down. Wynona could tell how angry I was and just stood there shaking. As calm as I could I took Angel's bags from Wynona. "I'm taking Angel and these bags to the car; I refuse to allow Mrs. Cary to get in this fight." We were going to handle this in private, tonight. I got behind the steering wheel filled with rage. How could she do this to me? Lord please help me, I don't want to be mean and ugly. You see I'm backed into a corner and I don't know which side of me will come out. Wynona finally came out walking slow. What the hell is this woman truly doing. ("I bet that ain't even yo baby." Woooooooo please get out of my head!)

As she got in the car Angel said, "Daddy I'm hungry, can we go get something to eat."

"Angel please shut up," Wynona shouted! I gripped the steering wheel so tight I could see blood form in my knuckles. Without any words being spoken I took Angel and her mom to Benny's. I asked Wynona did she want to eat in or carryout. She said, "We can eat in if that's ok with you." I grabbed two trays a preceded towards check in with Angel. I was fuming inside but I'm not going to be like the stereotyped black male showing off in public and making a spectacle of myself. Yes it hurt and I knew the war was raging; it was only a matter of time before the egg cracked, I could feel a huge fight coming.

We ate dinner in utter silence; even Angel was good for a change. She didn't ask for everything in the restaurant. Wynona and I made eye contact several times; she looked like she was scared as hell. I was allowing her to get her story together even though I knew what was going on. I have done everything to be a good husband and father to her child. Now it was time to find out why she had been lying to me all this time.

That night Wynona bathed Angel and put her to bed. I showered and sat quietly on the side of the bed waiting for her to get out the shower. She stayed in the bathroom longer than normal. I sat there, it was killing me inside. I wanted answers and I wanted them now. She came out in a night gown I had bought her. It was sexy but modest since she was pregnant. She was laying a trap thinking she would distract me with her lovely body and sex tonight but it wasn't going to work, Minnie Me had left the building. She came over to me and sat in my lap smelling of lavender and chamomile. She kissed me once then again; I lifted here off me and sat her on the end of the bed. She looked surprised that I would deny her since the pussy has been on lock down. I could only have it when she wanted to give it to me and it had to be her way or no way, meaning from the back; the quickest way known to man to get a nut, especially pregnant pussy. I had no control, pussy just felt so damn good. Maybe it was all those years of depriving myself, I don't know.

It felt strange to be in this position but I was about to man up. "Wynona I've had a few hours to think about what I want to say and how I would say this to you." ("Nigga you soundin' like a white boy.") "I just need to know what you're doing. What else are you hiding from me? Why didn't you tell me about Angel's dad being back in the picture and why did you have to lie on your own mother." The room was drop dead silent.

She got up and said, "Niggah please!"

Without thinking my hand went up so quick, she jumped and cleared her throat;

"First of all Ervin I didn't lie, you didn't ask anymore about her father so I didn't feel the need to discuss it with you."

"If you didn't lie, why did you pretend to be in your mom's house while I was there and she had no idea where Angel was?"

"Look nigga I said I didn't have to explain to you that she was spending time with her father."

"Wynona, I'm doing my best to keep from breakin' my foot off in your ass so please refrain from calling me a nigga again."

With a smirk look on her face she said, "After I have this damn baby a lot of things are gonna change."

Before I could blink the words spewed out my mouth. "Bitch, you can take your daughter and get the hell out now! Why wait, you don't give me no pussy, you treat me like shit and you expect me to be ok with all of it! Well I'm tired and you don't want to be here anyway, get the fuck out now! As a matter of fact, let me help yo ass to the door." ("Oh shit, did I miss something. I thought white boy was still talkin.") I grabbed her arm and moved her towards the door. She was screaming and hollering, "Let me get my shit."

I said, "What shit, you take what you came to me with, nothing; you leave with nothing.

She stood and looked at me harshly, "Are you serious Ervin, if I leave I will never come back and you won't have to worry about seeing your daughter"!

I was motionless, my daughter! She knew all this time it was a girl. "Wynona what do you want from me? I've given you the best that I have. I have loved your daughter like she was mine. You haven't wanted for anything but my best ain't good enough for you. What do you want, to be single again?"

Wynona sat on the front steps, "No Ervin, I just want us to be like every other couple. They do things together, they go out in groups, they attend concerts, they have a good time. All you want to do is work, work, work."

"Wynona if I don't work we don't eat. If I don't work we can't live in this big house. If I don't work I can't support you and my children. If I don't work I'll end up like some of those no good nigga's standing on the corner not taken care of their obligations. I'm a real man who believes in doing the right thing, going to work every day, coming home making sure my family has everything they need. We may not have everything we want but we do have all that we need. And if that is all your problem is why the hell you just now saying something? You want to act like a fool and bring me to the point of beatin' yo ass all because I work too much for you! You went to this extreme with lies on top of lies all because I work too much! All I asked you for is honesty, respect and love. When we first met you couldn't keep your hands off of me. I would be late going to work but I always left you satisfied and I couldn't wait to get home so we could do it all over again."

"Mike came over to my mom's place after he found out I got married and said he didn't want another man raising his daughter. He started giving me some money and asked could he see his daughter. At first I was scared of what you would think. I talked to my friends about it and they said you don't really have a say so because she has a daddy."

"Wynona, do you know how crazy you sound right now? I can understand Mike's point but why didn't you just come to me and tell me what was going on? That's what adults do, they communicate with each other. As for your ignorant so-called friends, all of them have kids and none of them are married; I wonder why that is! You chose to listen to street hoes over your own husband. Why did you feel the need to lie? Why is she always there, do you not like being a mother?"

"I thought if I let her spend time with her dad that would give you and I more time together. It didn't work cause you hardly spend any time with me." I sat down on the steps next to her.

I put my arm around her, at first I was hurt then I said, "If you don't want the life we have now I can go back to just having one job; we would have to give up everything else."

She said she was waiting for a good time to tell me but she had gotten a job offer as a social worker at the children's detention home. I was so surprised; I asked her when she was going to discuss it with me. She laid her head on my chest and shrugged her shoulders, tonight I guess. I laughed at her humor.

"When will you start, six weeks after the baby is born?"

"Yeah why didn't you tell me we were having a girl?"

"I sorta wanted it to be a surprise."

"Is that what you meant by a lot of things were going to change?"

"Yes, Ervin I said those things out of anger, will you forgive me please?"

"Wynona, we're going to iron out our differences. We're going to come together as one. If you want Angel to see her father on a weekly basis, I have no problem with that but I feel she's part of our family and she needs to spend the majority of her time with us; she's going to be a big sister."

"I apologize for hollering at you, I was so frustrated. Did you really mean for me to leave without nothing?"

I picked Wynona up and took her to bed. You know they say make up sex be the bomb.

Two weeks had passed and everything was pretty much back to normal. I was cleaning up the living room. I picked up a pile of mail and there was an envelope addressed to me. It had the United States Marine on the front of the package. My hands started to sweat; I ripped the envelope open, there was a picture and a note with a single address on it. I dropped to my knees saying thank you Jesus, it was a picture of the man I saw last at my graduation. We did look alike; the only difference he was a lighter shade of caramel than me. I looked at the address, Ernest Wyatt physical address was on the other side of town. He was living in the better part of Columbia SC. Wow it was amazing that we had never run into each other before.

Wynona came in the living room, "Ervin are you ok?"

"Yes honey I'm fine."

She knelt down beside me, "Ok, why are you crying."

"I just received some information as to where my father lives." I showed Wynona the picture, she said, "Damn you do look just alike!"

I shook my head and said, "Yes we do, it's funny when I look at the picture I see me when I get older." I helped her get up; she was big, much bigger this time around.

"What are you going to do now that you have this information?"

"I'm going to contact him at some point. I have to get the nerve to do it though. I don't handle rejection very well, you know that."

She said, "He came to your graduation and he has watched you in years passed. I say go and try to meet him, what could it hurt."

This was the first time in a long time that we agreed on something. Her normal approach was to fight me on everything from the kind of bread I bought to the little sleep wear outfits for the birth of our baby girl. Most times I would shake my head and walk away. I didn't want to nitpick about things like that; I just wanted my family to be happy. I set the picture and the address on the table.

Walking on the deck, the sun felt good on my face. There is a God who sits high and looks low and he knows just what you need and when you need it. I thanked Him for Molly, she didn't have to send this information; she was taking a huge risk by doing so and I asked God to protect her and let no harm or danger come to her.

"Ok lord, I have this information, now what do I do with it?" My first thought was to go out to his address and see where he lived then I would come up with a plan as to how I would meet him. Since I had nothing but time I decided to take a drive to look at the area and see how he was living. The thought of meeting my dad and spending real time with him stayed heavy on my mind. Not only did I want to have a personal relationship with him, I wanted my children to know there Grandpa, that's if in fact he is my father. I feel like he is, you never know.

As I rolled up on my dad's neighborhood I could see that the area was kept up very well and it was real quiet and peaceful. I didn't really see any children around so I figured it must be more of an older neighborhood. It turned out that his house was in a cul-de-sac so I acted like I was on the wrong street and just kept driving without stopping. From what I could see it was a single story ranch that sat several yards off the road with a double car garage on the right. The yard was well groomed with lots of trees and had some size to it. That's about all I could catch moving through the way I did without causing an accident.

On my way back across town I had a little smile of satisfaction on my face and I actually felt pretty good. Maybe I could get one of my friends to try and look up the address to make sure the property was his so I could be sure that I didn't waste my time going over there for nothing. The realization of just how easy this was turning out to be was beginning to settle in. All I needed to do now was decide when I wanted to take the next step and actually go to the door to meet him face to face.

Chapter 9

I was happy that I had become a father. My heart was overjoyed when my second daughter was born; she came into this world one sunny morning hollering at the top of her lungs. The doctor said she was perfect and so alert to be a few minutes old. I cried like I had her, she was the mirror image of me and her mother. Thinking of her birth brought tears to my eyes. Willow Alicia Wyatt came in weighting 8 pounds 9 and half ounces. I wanted nothing but the best for my children. It made me want to work even harder to make sure they had everything.

My Grandparents suggested that I have Willow baptized. I knew Wynona was going to fight me on this but I was going to at least approach her with the idea. One Saturday morning after Willow had turned three months old I told Wynona I wanted to talk to her about something important. She asked me could it wait, she wanted to go shopping with her friends. I explained that it was an important issue and we needed to discuss it together. She sat down huffing and puffing.

"I would like to have Willow baptized at my Grandparents' church."

Before I could say another word she said, "What the fuck for, I'm not going to that church with them and neither is Willow!"

"Wynona, I do have a say so in our daughter's life and I feel like she should be covered by baptism."

She stood up, her entire demeanor changed. She said, "Do what the fuck you want I'm out of here. ("Say man, when you gonna break yo foot off in her ignant ass?! I done had enough of this heffa talkin out the side of her neck at me." Sheeee's nooooot talkin to you.) I tried to reach out and touch her hand and she jerked away from me. I just left the situation alone for now. I consulted with my Grandparents and against everything Wynona said I told them I wanted my daughter to be baptized. I hadn't been to my Grandparents church since I was a young boy but I loved the idea of having it there; it would be a start. Grandma called me three days later and told me it would be on that coming Sunday. I looked at the calendar; it wasn't my weekend off but the baptism was going to be during the day. I just had to sacrifice my sleep time to see this take place.

I asked Grandma to find a pretty lil dress for Willow. She told me she would take care of everything. I made a few phones calls and invited a few family members and close friends. I even invited Crystal, even though I knew she probably wouldn't come.

My brother and his family was gonna be there and Wynona's mom, Ms. Cary, said she would love to come to the christening. Mom said she would even try to make it. Now the last person I had to convince was Wynona; again I had to catch up with her, she said her job was so demanding and that she didn't have time to breath. ("That's probably cause she got somebody's dick in her mouth." You know you really getting beside yourself.) I could understand the statement but you have to have time away from the job to take care of home; family is first and nothing comes before them but god almighty. I waited for her to get relaxed in the living room; she had just got off the phone talking to whoever. She seemed to be in a good mood. I sat down on the couch and asked her how her Saturday was going. She looked at me all weird like what the fuck you want now.

"It was going fine until you sat your ass down."

("If you don't snatch her damn wig off her head and punt her ass out the front door I'm..." Just chill for a minute please.) I took a deep breath and thought to myself, "She doesn't mean any ill against me." "Ok, well this won't take long and I'll be out of your way. "Tomorrow at 11:30 am is Willow's christening; you can come or I'll do it all by myself. Some of our family and friends plan to be there so it's your choice."

She got up off the couch and said, "Who gave you the right to do something like this behind my damn back?! I hate you!" and she stormed outside.

I wasn't going to let this demon stop me from having my child blessed; she was either going to join me or I was going to do it without her. ("Boy you...um.") I was the one who normally took care of everything in the house any damn way so it was gonna go my way tomorrow. I don't know what time I fell asleep but I got tired of waiting up for Wynona. It was 6 am; I went in the kitchen to get Willow a bottle and heard the front door open and shut. I looked around the corner to see Wynona's hair tossed all over her head. I just stared at her; she gave me a side smile and said, "I'm sorry I stayed out to late but I was really mad with you yesterday."

I walked past her like I didn't hear a word she was saying. My morning prayer was I wasn't going to argue with the devil and this was going to be a beautiful day. I fed Willow, burped and changed her, and she went back to sleep. I showered and got ready to go. I made sure to make a few bottles, packed diapers and a change of clothes for Willow after the christening. I didn't have to worry about Angel; her hair was already done so I woke her up, fed her and put her clothes on. This wasn't even my child but I loved her like she was mine.

The phone rang; it was Grandma asking was I running on schedule. I told her I was just about done and would be leaving in about a half hour. She said her and Grandpa would see us when we got to their house. I decided I would let Grandma dress her granddaughter in her christening outfit when we got to her house.

Just as I was strapping the baby in ready to leave Wynona came to the door screaming at the top of her lungs, "So you was just going to leave and not even ask me was I going."

"If you would care to remember, I told you yesterday that this was happening today at 11:30am and your uptight ass decided to stay out all night and get drunk." I clinched my teeth together for a second then politely said, "If you're going with us I will be leaving in five minutes with or without you." The door slammed shut; next thing I remember she had a bag in hand, comb sticking out her hair, one shoe on one off running toward the car; she had chosen some wrinkled ass dress from the closet and didn't take any time to press it. I said nothing. She tried to make small talk as I drove but I had very few words to say to her today day. I was really at a loss for words; what had I done to her? How did I end up with someone like this? Why couldn't she just be a sweet loving wife as she appeared to be when we were dating; we were so disconnected.

I could still smell the residue of alcohol on her breath as I pulled up to my Grandparent's home. I took the car seat out and Angel got out the car; even she was careful not to say anything. We walked up to the door and before we went in I took out a stick of gum and said, "You might want to chew this before you start speaking to people." She looked like she wanted to say something and that's when Grandpa opened the door and said, "I thought I heard someone coming up, get in here with my sweet granddaughter." I gave Grandpa the car seat and went off toward the living room. Angel held my hand as we walked together in the next room; Wynona tagged along.

Grandma came out and said, "Where's the sleeping Angel so I can dress her."

Wynona said, "I can help you."

Grandma looked at her and said, "Come on, let's get her ready for her big debut." She said she had bought the prettiest little christening outfit she could find.

Wynona picked up the baby and proceeded to take her clothes off. Grandma took over as Wynona watched her put more lotion on Willow's hands and legs. She turned her over and said, "Hmm, that's an odd birthmark, two cherries on her thigh."

Wynona said, "No that's not a birthmark that's her skin color that hasn't come in yet. Grandma finished dressing the baby in silence. Wynona seemed fearful of something and Grandma could sense it but this wasn't the time or place to address the issue. As both women came down stairs Angel said, "Here they come daddy." Angel moved so fast she tripped and fell and Wynona started hollering at her. I gave Wynona a look that stopped her in her tracks as I picked Angel up and kissed her knee. As I did that Grandma said, "Two cherries on her thigh as well." I put Angel down and just looked at Grandma; I didn't know what she was talking about. We all put our coats on and left for the christening.

Everyone who was invited was there including a few that weren't invited. The shocker was mom didn't make it so she sent Mr. Mike to represent her. I thought that was odd since they never hardly went anywhere together. For some reason Wynona kept looking over where everyone was sitting during the ceremony. Since she didn't have anything to do with planning the event I knew she wasn't expecting anyone. After the ceremony was finished I asked her who she was looking for during the christening. She played it off and said she thought my mom was gonna be there so she kept looking for her.

Everything ended well and we went home so I could get ready for work. I didn't get much rest that day and Wynona was no help at all. She wasn't a hands on mother and did as little as possible. She knew I was working hard; when I came through the door she would hand me the children then leave to go to work. We decided against nursery, daycare or even relatives taken care of our baby girl. I learned how to manage my time at home taking care of two little girls, cleaning, cooking and going to work. I would find myself sleeping with one eye open and one eye closed because Wynona all but refused to help me. She only took care of the children when I wasn't home.

The house would be a mess when I got there and instead of fussing I just did what I had to do for my girls who were growing like weeds. I picked up a third job and worked on the weekend as a correctional officer. This included going away once a month to do drill.

It had been some time since I last talked to Crystal; she called one day when I was on my way home from drill. As usual she was pleasant; she said she was just checking in on me. Why couldn't my wife be even the slightest bit like Crystal? I mean, who would have thought that things would turn out like this from the way things started out with us? We talked about everything and I kept her abreast of the children but I never told her I wasn't truly happy with my marriage. She would always listen to me and we would laugh, exchange pleasantries and then she was gone again. I always felt that empty feeling when she hung up.

When I got home from drill there was a note on the table saying the children were at my mom's house and that she was out with friends. Tired as I was I dropped my bags and headed towards my mom's house. All I could think about was how the hell did my girls end up at my mom's house of all places! I reached the door and my mom was bumping my baby girl to sleep, her speech was slurred as she said, "It's about damn time one of you showed up to get the children." My mom said Wynona dropped the children off right after I left for drill and never came back to get them. Wynona was getting beside herself with this shit. I thanked my mom, got my children and left. She was definitely in no shape to take care of my children and to think that she had them the entire weekend. Thinking about it as I drove made me even madder. Hell was she even sober at any point while the children were there? Aw fuck, what else may have happened over there in her drunken stuper? Aaaaaaaaaaaaaaa I can't go there right now, the thought just sickens me to even consider it.

Parenthood is hard enough but with me working three jobs, taken care of the children and having to deal with my non supportive wife/non-existent mother of my children, and the street hoe I call mom was wearing me out mentally. It's time I put my foot down; I was going to sit Wynona down and find out just what the hell was going on. ("Shiiiit, this I gotta see.")

Later that night Wynona showed up grinning like a Cheshire cat so I asked her to come and sit on the couch. I calmly remember asking her where she had been.

She stated to me it was none of my damn business. I barked back that it was my damn business because I was her husband.

She blurted out, "Not for long."

The silence after those words was like none I had heard before. I couldn't believe I was back at this point with her again.

As I somehow held my composure I asked, "What the fuck did you just say?"

She shook her head and said it was a poor choice of words.

"No, no, what you said was not a poor choice of words it was the truth being said." Instead of going with the thoughts flashing through my mind I got up and went to bed. There definitely was no love between the two of us anymore; where had I gone wrong. She came and got into bed; I bit my lip because I didn't want to fight with her but something was going to change. ("That's what I thought, punk nigga." Shut up!)

Wynona slide her hand under me and began rubbing on my dick. As hard as I tried to keep him down, this little nigga rose right up like the traitor he is. Although I really didn't want to I let her make love to me or should I say fuck me. I couldn't feel the passion that we had once upon a time. It was like she was doing it to keep me quiet. I rolled over on my side thinking what will happen next. I felt all alone at that moment and wished I could talk to Crystal; at least she made me smile and feel good about myself.

We didn't hardly speak for several months after that. It was the same routine, I would come in from working all night, she handed me the baby and I would feed and bathe her, get my oldest daughter off to school and the baby and I would get in the bed and sleep until my oldest got out of school. I was also the one keeping the house clean because she barely lifted a hand to do anything. She would leave for work not returning until she knew it was time for me to leave for my next shift for work.

After hardly speaking for several months I came home one day to a clean house, the baby wasn't thrown in my arms and the house smelled good. I could actually smell something cooking in the kitchen. Do I have to tell you how shocked I was!

Wynona told me to take a load off my feet; she was actually looking like the woman I married. Something was wrong, I could feel it. I knew she was setting the stage to tell me something. Was it those words "not for long" coming back to haunt me.

She bathed the children and put them to sleep, gave me a massage, which I hadn't felt her hands on me in months. Now I was really starting to think this is some kind of Sealy moment in reverse or something. One thing led to another and, as tired as I was, we had what they call relations. I say that because it felt empty, there was no passion or love, but I did it because I'm her husband. I was concerned for I knew there was more to this little performance to come.

I braced myself for the worst. Then it happened. She said, "We needed to talk."

I leaned up on one arm looking in her eyes; I was trying to read her. She explained that she had been a real bitch here lately and that she was going to do better. She said after our second daughter was born she was having a tough time with her hormones.

I told her I could understand that, this does happen but it still didn't explain how she was acting. She said there was one more thing she needed to tell me.

I said, "Ok I'm listening."

She took a little box off the dresser and told me to open it. I hesitated at first then I opened the box and saw a pair of little white booties in the box. I looked at her puzzled; was she really trying to tell me we were expecting another child? Our daughter was just nine months old. A part of me was overjoyed but the other part of me was sick. Was it even my baby, had she been cheating on me out there shaking her ass and hanging in the club? We hadn't made love before tonight in three months. I chose my words very carefully, "Wow ("Whose fuckin baby you carrying," was the thought that flashed.) we are pregnant again?"

She began to smile. I asked her was she sure she wanted to have this child knowing she had a rough time after the second baby and willow was not yet a year old. Wynona got upset and said if I didn't want the baby just say so.

It wasn't that I didn't want the child I just knew I couldn't handle a third child by myself. I would need her to help and do her part as their mother and my wife. We cried and held each other, and prepared to bring yet another life into the world.

Chapter 10

Time passed quickly, Wynona was six months pregnant. Crystal called while I happened to be washing dishes. She was her usual self just checking on me and the family. I told her we were expecting another baby in three months. She was glad and said life had been going good for me. I finally asked her, "How are you doing, what's going on in your life?" It finally dawned on me that she had said very little about her personal life during any of our conversations. How could I have been so thoughtless not to ask about her all this time, was I that far gone? ("Aaaaaaa ha ha ha, niggah you still gone.")

She said she was a worship leader in her church and that she was saving herself for her husband. She had finished college and received her PHD. I was so happy for her, she was a psychologist now. I told her maybe if time permitted one day we could get together and celebrate her getting her degree. She said that would be fantastic!

I had to admit, Wynona tried hard to come home right after work. She even tried to help me more. Some days when I came home things were a little untidy but she managed to keep things together. She wasn't a very good cook so I took it upon myself to cook for our family every day before I went to sleep. If it were left up to her we would have sandwiches every day. I was a meat and rice kind of man. I also knew she was eating for two so she needed good meals. She was due around Willows first birthday so we were undecided as to whether to have a big party or not because we weren't sure when the baby would arrive.

My life was hard to explain if someone were to ask me how things were. I knew I loved my wife but I had uncertainties as to whether I was in love with her; she had put a wedge between us so my state of mind was hard to explain. Also being a typical man I wondered whether my wife had been unfaithful. Normally when she talked to her friend girl's she didn't mind that I heard their conversations. Then there were times she would be talking and I pretended to be sleep and she would speak very low. She would get up and go in the bathroom or into another room and talk. I shook my head because I didn't want to act ugly.

This particular Friday when I got off I knew I didn't have to report back to work until Monday. It was one of the rare times I was off from all three jobs. I called Crystal's number and got her answering service. I left a message saying, "Hey Crystal if you're free tonight let's go out for that drink I promised you!" I wasn't sure whether she would call back but I was going to prepare myself to go out anyway. Wynona was seven and a half months pregnant; she wasn't at risk or anything. I needed a break and I desperately wanted to just go out. We were friends and I owed her a drink.

I had just reached the house and my phone rang. I looked at the incoming call, it was Crystal. "Hello Crystal how are you doing for a Friday?" She said all was well. She said she could meet for drinks around seven if it wasn't going to be a problem for me or my wife. I bristled at the thought and chuckled lightly, "No Crystal all is well on the home front. I wouldn't have called if I thought it would be." She said ok! We talked for about an hour more.

I went in the house and found Wynona sitting in the front room looking crazy. She said, "Who was you talkin to out there for so long?"

"You know, a normal wife would say something like, "Good morning baby how was work?," or meet me at the door with a beautiful smile, kiss and a hug, but no, I got to have the bitch wife asking me who I was talkin to for so long. I got enough to deal with at work, I don't need to come home and hear more shit from you."

"I want to know who you was talkin to?"

"If it was any of yo damn business you would know but since it ain't yo business you can get the fuck out my face and mind your own damn business. You got nerve askin me shit like that anyway with yo creepin ass sneakin off into other rooms to talk to whoever you talk to "IN PRIVATE" so I can't hear what you're saying. Yeah, I know every time that damn phone rings and when you get yo ass up and walk out. So you tell me miss yuck mouth, who the hell you be talkin to so mutha fuckin early in the morning "IN PRIVATE" all the time? Don't you dare try to lie to me and say it's one of your friend girl's cause you don't talk sexy to no girls. You fuckin around on me Wynona?" ("Wow, now that was a switch up fo yo ass, haha. Answer that one biatch!")

Wynona froze in her tracks and didn't know what to say. Then she said, "How you gonna ask me something like that and I'm almost eight months pregnant with your fuckin baby? I can talk to whoever I want to whenever I want to, niggah!"

"My point exactly; niggah."

She grabbed a few things along with Angel and went out the door; it didn't matter to me where she was going as long as it was away from me. Willow was still sleeping thank goodness so I locked up and took a shower. Finally a little peace; I didn't hear Willow moving yet so I laid down for a few. Getting out for a few was going to be good for me; I hadn't seen Crystal in a minute anyway and all the stress around me was beginning to build up so I needed relief bad.

I woke up to peaceful calm and had the biggest stretch ever. I got up and went in to check on Willow who was playing in her crib. I said hello and kissed her little forehead, then changed her diaper, grabbed her up and off we went into the kitchen. It was a little after noon and Wynona still hadn't shown up so I gave my little princess a bath, made lunch and laid her down for a nap. Later in the day I took Willow over to my Grandparent's house. Grandma always had a wonderful time playing with her. Of course Grandpa and I did our usual thing and talked on the front porch and drank tea. It was always so peaceful over there and I didn't have a concern for anything. Grandpa asked where Wynona was and I told him about our little session of words earlier. I told him she left with Angel earlier that morning and that I hadn't seen or heard from them since. He cautioned me to be careful with her during this time and said things would get better soon. Grandma fixed dinner and we all ate; I could never get enough of eating her food.

It was getting close to my meeting time with Crystal so I asked if Willow could spend the night and Grandma disappeared with her. I looked at Grandpa and said, "I guess that was a yes." We laughed and said our goodbyes.

I had a little time to kill so I went back to the house and got ready for my evening out; we decided to meet at Appletree's. I had an unusual smile on my face. I was happy for a change. I thought to myself, I'm just going to go have drinks, what harm could come of two friends having drinks.

I arrived at Appletree's on time and Crystal was there waiting for me. The night went so well. All I could think about was how good I felt just being around someone that truly liked being in my company. We talked about everything just like we used to when we were young. After a few hours we decided it was time to go and said our goodbye. I asked if it would be alright to do this again sometime. She smiled and said she would love to. All I needed to do was let her know when.

The ride home was so peaceful and I didn't have a worry on my mind at all. After arriving at the house, I went in and noticed the lights and TV were on. I walked in the living room; no one was there. I went into the girl's room and no Angel. I went in our bedroom; Wynona was nowhere to be found. I looked for a note, there was none? I looked at my phone, there were no missed calls. I knew Wynona had been there cause she left the TV and lights on but it wasn't like her to leave them on when she left the house. She had just had a Doctor's appointment two weeks ago and wasn't due to return until she was eight months, and was off on Fridays. I paced the floor for about an hour trying to make since of where she could be. It was too late to go looking around so I showered and went to bed.

The next morning I got up and things were still the same; no one was there but me. I got dressed and went to my Grandparent's house. I walked through the front door;

they never locked the doors. I shook my head, older people need to change their ways leaving the door open. I walked into the living room; my Grandpa was sitting in his favorite chair asleep, mouth wide open. I tipped by him and smelled something cooking in the kitchen. Reaching the kitchen my Grandma had her back to me getting something out the refrigerator. Willow was sitting at the table and hadn't noticed me yet. I didn't want to frighten Grandma so I just stood there; as she was turning around she said in a high pitch voice, "Someone gonna shoot you boy scaring me half to death." That's when Willow saw me and I went over to kiss her. Grandma's grin was so wide I could see how she had aged over the years but she was still so beautiful and of course feisty.

"What brings you over here so early, is everything ok at home?"

My Grandma was a good woman; she had always given me good sound advice. I needed to talk to her and Grandpa; they were my parents for real, they had always been there for me.

"Grandma, have you heard from Wynona today or last night?"

She stood still and shook her head, "I can't say that I have, why what's wrong son?"

"Well I got home from work yesterday and we had a little fall out. She left the house with Angel shortly after and I haven't seen or heard from them since. I came in early this morning to find the lights and TV on in the living room but no Wynona or Angel."

"Son maybe she went to the grocery store or something."

"Grandma, she would've left me a note. Today is her normal day off." We pondered over the thought of where she could be at this hour while we ate and talked, then Grandpa comes in.

He said he knew he smelt food cooking in the kitchen. He looked at me and smiled, "When did you sneak in here boy?"

I said, "While you were sitting in your favorite chair with your mouth wide open calling the hogs in for breakfast."

We all bust out laughing. He sat down and Grandma put his plate in front of him. He was eating a midday breakfast of ham, eggs, home fried potatoes and coffee. Grandma left the kitchen with Willow. He began to scoop the eggs and fried potatoes in his mouth, then looked up at me and just stared as he chewed. "He said, "What's wrong son, I can see it all over your face." My Grandpa knew me to well.

I explained how I came home this morning to find the lights and TV on but no Wynona or note left for me.

He said, "Maybe she went to the store."

Old people! I adamantly shook my head no, "She would've left a note for me and she left the lights and TV on in the living room; she never does that. She's good about turning things off if she goes out. I know we had a few words yesterday and it's her day off but still Grandpa!" He asked me had I called some of her women friends.

I said, "No the last time I did something even remotely close to this Wynona and I argued for almost two months, she said she wasn't a child and I didn't need to be checking up on her."

"Ok son, I understand she may feel like that but she's in the motherly way. Anything could've happened so it's your damn business right now. Now I told you from the very beginning I didn't really care for how you done things with her so I have tried to stay out of it. I know you ain't happy son."

I stared off into space listening but also absorbing his every word. "You aren't happy," how does he know, is it written all over my face. I thought I had gotten good at hiding my feelings from everyone. I hung around my Grandparents' home for another hour then I went back home. As I was turning onto our street I saw a black sedan with tinted windows backing out my drive way. I tried to speed up to the house but the sedan went in the opposite direction.

I got Willow out and went in the house. After putting Willow in her crib I asked Angel to stay in the room with her sister. I proceeded towards the bedroom and found Wynona getting out the shower. I just stood there, she looked up and saw me standing there and said I startled her.

"Wynona, why would I startle you, I'm your husband and I live here right?"

I could feel my blood pressure rising. "Where the hell have you been and who the hell was that leaving out our driveway when I was pulling in."

She looked at me all crazy and said she had no idea what I was talking about. I asked again, "Where have you been Wynona?" She just stood there looking crazy.

At that moment Angel came up behind me and said, "We was at Mike's house all night daddy, he told me to shut the fuck up and go to sleep." Wynona screamed, "Go to your room Angel you don't know what you're talkin bout!"

They say from the mouths of babes the truth comes out. I whirled around to face my daughter, she looked so innocent and I knew she was telling me the truth. Baby girl go in your room and play with Barney, I'll come in and get you in a little bit. She said, "Ok Daddy give me a hug since Mike wouldn't hug me last night before I went to sleep."

"Wynona, before you say another word think real hard about what you gonna tell me because if it ain't the truth all hell is gonna break out in here." As I stood in her face, I was so close to her I could almost hear her heart beating.

She said, "Well you see what had happen was after what you said I took Angel and went to the store. I called my friend girl to come get us but she was having car trouble so I called my friend guy Mike to come get us. He said it was so late so he invited me back to his house until we could get my friend girl to come get us."

"You want me to believe that tired ass story? You must think I'm so fuckin' stupid that I don't know that you're lying to me. So, let me see if I got this right. You was pissed off and took Angel to the store. Wow, you didn't drive so who took you to the store and couldn't bring you back home? ("Yeah, who took you to the fuckin' sto?") You called your girl to pick you up but she couldn't so the next nigga you call is your ex rather than your husband to come get you. Why didn't you call me or my Grandparents?

"Well you see, I did call you but it went straight to voice mail. I thought you turned the phone off and didn't want to talk to me."

"So why didn't you call my Grandparents?"

"I lost their number."

"You know what, I'm gonna stop right here cause I'm bout to do something that you ain't gonna like at all." This bitch is lying. If it wasn't for her being pregnant I would knock her damn teeth out her mouth. I backed up cause I needed some air. The room was starting to reek of nothing but lies and betrayal. "Why are you still messing with Mike and why is it he was the only number that was convenient to you? Why didn't he just bring you home?"

She said, "Look mutha fucka, I done told you what happened. You can believe me or not that's your damn problem."

She brushed pass me. I grabbed her arm and snatched her to me. "First of all, I'm not ya Mutha fucka, I'm your husband. When I got home and you weren't here there was a cause for me to be alarmed because you left no note and it appeared that you left in a hurry. Then I drive up to my house and a black sedan is leaving my driveway; on top of that our daughter said you all spent the night at this mutha fucka's house. And to make matters worse he told my daughter to shut the fuck up and go to sleep. Now what was it that he didn't want her to be awake to see? You also said my daughter didn't know what she was talking bout. Now, you can do whatever the hell you like with Angel but you will not leave here with my daughter. It's time for you to go." I pushed her away.

She slipped on some stretch pants, a big shirt and was standing in front of me looking like she just got caught with her hand in the cookie jar.

"Did you sleep with him?" She threw a bottle of lotion at me and stormed out the room. "Make sure you don't stop anywhere else in the house. The door is right there and you can have your sedan friend come pick you up again."

She slammed the door and walked off. ("Now that's my niggah. You still shoulda knocked that bitch out." Shut up man.)

Sitting on the bed I was tired and drained from all that had taken place. All I wanted to do was wake up and find that I had been dreaming the whole time. I picked up the phone and called my Grandparents. I told Grandma that Wynona was home when I got back. She asked where she had been. She said, "She shouldn't scare you like that knowing she's getting ready to have that baby soon." I just shook my head and listened. After she calmed down I thanked her for listening to me. I told her I would come by the house soon and give her and my Grandpa all the details. I sat thinking about meeting Crystal for drinks again. I needed it more than ever today. Before going to bed I made sure to use all the locks on the doors and checked to make sure the windows were locked. I knew she didn't have all the keys.

Chapter 11

That night I drifted off into a deep sleep. For as long as I could remember, my recurring dream was of a romantic liaison in a public place. The fear of discovery intensifies the sexual tension coursing through my veins. Imagine making love to someone just yards away from detection. If I think about it long enough, I can almost see her approaching now. The sun at her back casts a shadow over her facial features, but I have no doubt who she is. This woman has plagued my erotic dreams for years. I'd know that silhouette anywhere. As she draws closer, I can make out her features; the light piercing eyes, her perfect smile, and the way her brows raised ever so slightly as she approaches. Her fluid stride is that of a woman who knows what she wants as she stalked her prey, waiting for the perfect moment to move in for the thrill.

I try to will my body not to move, but her gaze has me quivering from head to toe. I can feel my pulse racing, that familiar ache spreads from the core of my body reaching out in all directions, turning my blood to fire. My uncontrolled body has taken on a life of its own. I instantly know that only this bronze Queen can quench the inferno within me. Deep down I know my reaction to this woman makes no since, but I also realize that only she can put out the blaze that's threatening to consume my mind, body, and soul.

With a nod of her head I lead her to a secluded area behind several tall bushes. There my hands begin their sensuous exploration of her body, slowly, purposely stroking her skin. I feel the heat wherever I touch her. It felt as if I'd spontaneously combust if I don't make love to her soon. I see her bite her lip to suppress the scream threatening to tear itself from her mouth. I slowly remove my jacket and gently lay her down on it. I remove her blouse, caressing her nipples until they press firmly against my hand. Lord help me this woman is playing my body like a tightly strung violin. I noticed the sweet smile upon her lips as we came together in a passionate kiss. I felt a sudden rush course through my entire body, it took my breath away. I withdraw to remove my shirt. Looking into her eyes I felt her nipples again beneath my fingertips. She slowly stroked my washboard abs, drinking in my chiseled form. Her body looks as if it's been carved out of a slab of solid mahogany and finished into a true masterpiece. As she continues her assault on my senses, I feel the cool breeze on my chest. ("It's the ceiling fan niggah, wake up.")

I skillfully strip the rest of my body effortlessly in one fluid motion, removing pants, socks, and shorts. This was no unskilled youth groping her body in the park. I'm working her like a master mechanic fine tuning a high powered Ferrari and she has my engine red lining. If it continues on too much longer I might blow a gasket. I look in amazement at her body. There's not a single flaw to be seen anywhere. It's like someone opened the girl-toy catalog and ordered one with extra everything. The next thing I know she's kissing my chest again, working her way to my nipples. Her tongue makes contact as she moves past my navel. I soon realize that I'm in for the time of my life as she determined to give me the same pleasure that I've shown her. She works her way to the main course. I started to breathe quickly as she takes me into her mouth. Her tongue can be sinfully addictive, my dick and the world begins to spin. Her sucking motion has my body quivering with anticipation.

My instinct suddenly demands that I not be selfish and tells me to allow her to share in more of my pleasure zone. After all this isn't a man's world alone! As she was working her erotic magic on me I slowly moved my hand between her thighs and began gently running my fingers around her clit. She instantly began to moan and move her body as if she were slow dancing. The more of her I discover, the more I want. The aroma of her flowing caramel was intoxicating. Unable to take anymore I pull her on top of me and let her slowly take me in to heaven. From this vantage point I can feel the pleasure of my dick going in and out of her juicy pussy. I wanted her to control the depth and the speed of our love making while I watched her climb higher and higher to ecstasy. She stroked me almost into a love comma. She sat up on top of me with her head back, exposing that sweet clit of hers to me. My hand slid down under her and as I played with her button she begin grinding on me hard until she came all over me. As the tension mounted again I smoothly roll her onto her back, effectively regaining control of the situation. Being somewhat of a stranger to the game, I could tell she was a first class lover. I brought both her knees up to the sides of her chest so I could get maximum exposure to her G-Spot. She was open like an early morning flower taking in all the sunlight. She began shaking uncontrollably as our mutual orgasm takes hold. As we exploded her legs gripped my body like a vice and the sounds coming from her were almost primitive; the wetness covering both of us.

As we lay there afterwards, gasping for breath, time seems to stand still. Neither of us wants to move, but discovery is eminent, so rise and dress. Suddenly the fog clears and I realize that I'm still dreaming. This whole event was just a mid-day fantasy. In getting up I noticed I was wet; did I just have a wet dream? I couldn't do anything but laugh at myself. I can't wait to see Crystal for drinks. In my heart I know I wouldn't actually act upon my dream or fantasy but it sure felt good. ("This niggah pussy wiped in a dream too. What da hell!")

I got up, took a shower and went searching through the house. Angel and Willow were still sleeping like little Angels. What has really gone wrong, why didn't I see any of this coming with Wynona? The house was still locked up and there was no sign of her anywhere. Oh well! Aw damn, spoke to soon. Yeah Wynona was back, she never went anywhere. I found here asleep in the car; damn!

Crystal and I met again for drinks that night. I felt a little guilty but what the fuck Winona had done this to me countless times and I needed time alone. She had really grown into a beautiful woman, nothing like I remember as a big head youngster trying to get some pussy. Her eyes were the same light piercing eyes that looked like they could see straight through you. She stood 5'10," her skin was Mahogany brown, her breast were full but small, her waist line was tiny, she had full hips and her butt looked firm. ("Ka-daiyam.") She smelled like an exotic honeysuckle. Her hair was a mixture of spice cognac and brown, she wore it straight. Her smile said it all; she was glad to be here and right now so was I, relaxed.

We talked and laughed, I showed her pictures of my two most special girls Angel and Willow. She said Willow looked like my mini me. I thought, "She looks like my dick! Oh, she looks LIKE me." Yeah, I thought that as well.

I asked Crystal could I ask her something personal. She said, "Go ahead ask away."

"Do you want children?"

"Yes, I want them Ervin but I have to have a husband first right?" She hit my arm.

"Are you dating anyone?"

She looked at me and gave me a long stare, "Truthfully speaking I haven't had the time to date. I've been so busy looking for a Job and working in my church."

"I can understand that. You're a beautiful woman; I just think you should be moving toward that, you aren't getting any younger."

"So you saying I'm about to be an over the hill old hag soon?" I bust out laughing and told her that's not what I meant.

She said, "Now let me ask you a question or two."

"I said, "Shoot." "Do you and your family attend church?"

I bust out laughing again. "No, Wynona in church, right! We don't but I'm a spiritual person. I read the word and I love God. I thank him every day for my life!"

"This next question is important but you don't have to answer it if you feel I'm over stepping my bounds. Are you happy in your marriage?"

Wow, didn't see that Mack truck coming and I was standing in the middle of the street. "Where did that question come from?" A hot flash ran through me and I got a little nervous at that moment. Do I really tell her what's going on or wait till later?

"Ok, since you asked a question without answering my question I'll tell you why I asked. Ervin, I have known you for quite some time and I've spoken to you over the phone countless times; you have never really mentioned your wife to me. You always say what you've done but you never say what you two do together. When a man is happy in his marriage he speaks of the love he has for his wife at some point and he makes sure others can see the love that lies deep inside. I'm being truthful I don't see that when you talk to me."

Her words hit like a ton of bricks and out of nowhere, all the anger from Wynona's bullshit came flooding in. "Ok, I see Ms. Foster, you're using your doctor skills on me." She giggled but her facial expression never wavered. Now how was I going to answer this question without falling apart, we would be here all night.

"I…love my wife and children very much. A marriage is something you work on daily and like they say we die daily. I feel a part of the marriage dies daily as well so you have to fight hard to keep it alive."

"Good answer Ervin but you still haven't answered me totally. I'm going to leave it alone until another time."

"Good cause I was starting to sweat, I thought you might have me lay on that bench over there."

We both laughed, I could've sat there and talked to her all night. I didn't want the night to end. Appletree's was closing. I was a little embarrassed keeping her out as long as I did. We walked out the restaurant and as we approached her car we both started to speak at the same time. I told her to go ahead, she said, "No you go ahead."

I looked at her and said, "I hope this isn't the last time we see each other."

She smiled, "Ervin, even though you're not saying right now, I know something is going on with you and I don't like to see you in pain. You and I will always be friends and I know that you know we share a special bond."

We both looked at each other as if we knew what the other was thinking. I wanted to tell her everything but this wasn't the right time. I knew once I started the water would come along with the anger and..., this just wasn't the right time.

She put her hand on my chest and said, "I know we'll stay in touch, just call me like you did this time."

I stood there thinking to myself - damn I don't want her to go. Who was I kidding, I had a whole set of new problems at home I had to deal with. I knew I couldn't mess her life up a second time. We hugged and said our good byes. I hugged her so tight, it felt good and it felt right. We both knew there was something special about our friendship.

I got in my car and headed in the direction of home. I looked at the clock; it was two in the morning. Time really flies when you're having a good time. I pulled out my phone and noticed Wynona had called me a half dozen times.

I thought back about what had taken place with Wynona and it hit me all at once. Mike was Angel's father! ("Duh, stupid!") I don't know if it was the stress from the situations mixed with working like I do or what but I completely missed it. She has been getting with this niggah the whole damn time. ("Aaah, you think, hello!") I hope she ain't pregnant by this bastard. ("Oh, now you want to hear me, I told yo dumb ass that months ago!" Man why don't you shut up.) Wynona better not be running no game on me.

I raced home mad as hell. I was 99 percent sure that the Mike Angel was talking about was her daddy. Wynona may not have even told Angel he was her father. I guess cause Angel always called me daddy and not him.

My hands trembled as I opened the door. The house was quiet, I started walking down the hallway toward the bedroom and a light came on in the living room.

Wynona said, "Where have you been Ervin, I've been calling you for God knows how long."

I stopped for a moment; I really don't think she was wanting to go there with me right now. At this moment I needed to know was that Mike's black Sudan that pulled out our yard that day. Standing there a few moments speechless, I mumbled something and kept walking towards the bedroom. To be almost eight months pregnant, I could hear Wynona moving fast behind me.

"I know you heard me Ervin, where the hell have you been."

I stood there a moment glaring down at her. She appeared to have been crying; good for her ass. She needs to feel some of the pain I've felt over the past couple of years. I walked in the room and put my keys on the dresser. I started taking my shirt off totally ignoring her. Wynona came close to me as my back was turned and dug her nails into my skin. I whirled around and slapped her across her face. She fell on the bed screaming and kicking at me. She kicked me in the groin and that was the last straw. I said, "If you get up off that bed acting crazy, I'm gonna show you what rage feels like." I should've seen the signs long ago. I could feel blood coming down my back.

Wynona jumped up again, this time she had my club in her hand. Her footing was unstable and she had this vile look on her face.

"Woman, if you attempt to hit me with that club, we'll both die in here tonight. Try me!"

I don't know what my face looked like but she must have saw it cause she thought long and hard about what I said. She stood there a few minutes and then ran in Angel's room shouting, we're getting the hell out of here and we're never coming back.

I yelled up the hall, "You not gone yet! Just remember, you only take what's on your back, everything else stays including my Willow."

She came to the door of the bedroom yelling, "I bought things too."

"What, a couple of t-shirts, some make-up and a few pair of shoes." I walked up the hall, grabbed her by the arm and took her to the front door. Angel was crying as Wynona drug her along. I opened the door and put her out. As she tried to speak I looked down at Angel and said, "I will always love you and be here for you my little Angel. You might not understand now but we'll see each other again. You be good and don't worry. Everything will be ok."

Wynona looked at me like she could scratch my eyes out. I told her if she did anything on her way off the property I would have her locked up. I shut the door in her face, locked the door and walked off. I grabbed a towel and went in the bathroom. I needed to assess the damage she inflicted on my back. Turning to the mirror I had six gashes in my back; blood was trickling out of all of them. I needed to go to the hospital even though I got tetanus shoots last year. I want to make sure infection from those fake nails didn't set in my back. I put a dark t-shirt on to keep anyone from noticing; I put a bag together for Willow and rapped her up. I grabbed my keys off the dresser, picked up the bag and we headed toward the front door. When I opened the door Wynona was still standing there.

"Ervin, I'm so sorry I hurt you, I didn't mean it. You just make me so damn angry sometimes."

"Wynona, I don't care how angry you make me, I have never resulted to violence and I'm sure as hell not going to start now. You can leave, I don't give a damn what you do anymore!

"Ervin, my children and I need you."

"You should've thought about that before you lost your mind. You come in this house from God knows wherever and you lie about where you've been. Then I hear from Angel who tells me exactly where you've been. When I ask for the truth you run in Angel's room and try to hide. I go out and have a few drinks then come home and you act like you so damn concerned. Then you scratch the living shit out of me and now you need me. What the fuck kind of drugs are you on. I can't take this shit anymore. We need to go our separate ways."

I closed the door and left her standing there. I'm finished trying to be a good husband to her. I gently put Willow in her car seat then sat in the car a few moments making sure she didn't do anything crazy and to get my mind right. Taking out my cell I held it out the window and said, "Do I need to call 911 or what?" She said fine and walked off. I called my friend, if she answered fine; if she didn't that was fine too.

The phone rang three times; on the fourth ring I was about to hang up when a sleepy Crystal answered the phone. She said hello several times before I spoke up. "Crystal it's me Ervin. I apologize for calling you like this but I need a friend right now."

The line was silent, "What do you need Ervin? I'll do my best to help in any way I know how."

"I need to see you now; can I come to your house?"

"Erivn, I'm not sure that's a good idea."

"Please Crystal, I'm not trying to be slick, I need you right now; I'll explain once I get there."

She gave me her address and I knew exactly where she stayed. I pulled up to her house and saw a single light on. I grabbed Willow and bag, went to the door and rang the doorbell; Crystal answered. Her hair was wrapped in a scarf and she had on a pair of shorts and t-shirt, "Come in."

I said, "Thank you, this is my little Willow."

She took her from me and said, "She is beautiful and looks just like you." She showed me to her living room and laid Willow down so she could continue resting. "Have a seat Ervin. Now what's so important that you couldn't wait until morning or that you couldn't talk about over the phone."

I hadn't noticed that I was shaking and as tears began streaming down my face I turned away from her. I heard her gasp, "Oh my God what's goin on Ervin!"

"I'm not sure where to begin. This has been going on for so long and the anger in me has become unbearable. Wynona just pushed me over the top tonight and I had to leave before I did something bad to her. Just lift up my shirt and you'll see what I mean."

She lifted my shirt and said, "Oh my god this is bad Ervin." I just stood there in silence. She left the room and a few minutes later came back caring everything she needed to attend to my wounds. She laid a sheet and towel down and instructed me to lie down on the couch. She said softly, "Ervin you have to take this shirt all the way off." I carefully lifted the shirt above my head as part of it was sticking to my back. Our eyes met briefly, I could see the love in her eyes. She looked away for this was not the time but I knew right then this is where I truly belonged.

It took a couple hours for her to clean the wounds. She was so patient and caring. I felt like there was a blaze in me and I couldn't put it out. With each touch of her hand she slowly kindled the rage within me and put me at peace. She never said a word. When she finished I sat up; Crystal retreated to a big chair on the other side of the room. I looked at her with love and compassion. "Thank you for helping me."

"You're welcome Erivn, now do you care to tell me what transpired for her to reach this level of rage with you?"

I looked at the clock on the wall and smiled, "Do you have time?"

"Yes, I have nowhere to go at the moment." Her smile made me want to drink her like a tall glass of sweet tea.

"Ok, I came in from having drinks with you. I was headed to the bedroom to shower and lay down. Before I made it to the room she starts questioning me about where I had been. I continued on to the room without saying anything and that's when all hell breaks loose. She asked me where I had been again and I ignored her. I didn't feel like arguing with her so I turned my back and she came up behind me and dug her nails in my back."

"It's more like she mauled you she was really angry with you. Had you ever gone out for drinks before with a friend?"

"No Crystal, this was only my second time going out with anyone and that was you."

"What really made you go out for drinks?"

"Aaaaaaaa Crystal, I just needed some air and I knew I promised you drinks for getting your degree. I didn't want to be with anyone else and I knew being around you would be as lovely as it always is. So I figured what better time than now."

Crystal raised her eyebrows and said, "I don't believe this is the entire story as to why you went out but I'm going to let it go for now. Now that you're all bandaged up, what do you plan to do?"

"If it's ok with you I'd like to stay right here on your couch until day break and then leave."

"It's cool with me Ervin. I'm going to say this and I'll never speak on the subject ever again unless you become my client."

We both laughed. "I'm listening."

"You're a good man and I can see you care about your family, however, if you're not happy in your marriage seek counseling. Anyone that will fly into a rage like your wife has done is not to be trusted; there are some deep rooted issues that need to be addressed."

"Thank you Crystal, I appreciate everything you've done. There are some issues that do need to be addressed and I have to handle it. I just have to wait it out a little longer. I just don't want to burden you with all my problems."

Crystal went and got a blanket, she said, "Good morning my friend." She kissed me on the forehead and off she went into, I presume, her bedroom.

As I lay on the couch there was no doubt in my mind she was my true soul-mate. I saw the gaze in her eyes. When I'm close to her my body burns like an inferno. I knew she was the one I could truly fall in love with. Just seeing her eyes swell with tears looking at my back spoke volumes to me. Her sensuous touch on my back made my pulse race and made a familiar ache spread through my body. I dreamt about that woman making my body quivering from head to toe again.

Chapter 12

The next morning I found a piece of paper and left a note. "We are friends for life, thank you for being here for me and not judging me or my situation. I'll be in touch, your true friend indeed. Ervin."

Driving home I thought about Crystal's touch and what she did to my body. I needed to shut it down for now. I had to go home and deal with this marriage. As I drove my thoughts again went to what happened and how Wynona went into a rage. Did I want to deal with something like this for the rest of my life? Did I make a hasty decision by marrying her? ("Ah, I can name that note in one word dummy. Yep!") Was there more to this entire episode? I parked the car and got out. A part of me wished when I opened the door that this was all a dream and she would be waiting to greet me when I walked in. I didn't want her to try and take Willow but this sorta thing happens every day. I was prepared for the worst.

Well I guess I don't have to say no one was in the house. I went in the living room and put Willow in her play pen. She stood up and clapped her hands. She fell down, got her bottle and threw it out of the playpen. I guess this was the "Get me something to eat" sign. Willow was my pride and joy; I loved Angel but there was a special connection with me and Willow. I picked her up and headed toward the kitchen to fix her a bottle. She was probably hungry but a bottle would do until I could get myself squared away.

I pulled Willow's playpen in the room, laid her down with the bottle and jumped in the shower. I was careful to make sure I didn't get my back wet. After I finished, I put my clothes on and heard a knock at the door. I went to see who it was and there stood Wynona and Angel. I opened the door and said, "What do you want!"

"Ervin, I really didn't mean to hurt you, I just wanted to know where you were last night I'm so sorry." She started to cry.

This always tore at my heart, Lord please fix these problems. I motioned for her to come in and closed the door behind them. Angel grabbed my leg and said, "Daddy, I want to be with you, please don't make me leave." I dropped to my knees and hugged her as a tear ran down my cheek. This was really getting to me now.

I quickly wiped my face, stood and told Wynona to have a seat on the couch while I checked on Willow and left her and Angel in the room together. When I returned I said, "I heard what you said but you can't take your anger out on the one you claim to love. Suppose I had gone into a rage when I saw that car leaving our house and you just stepping out the shower. How do you think I felt? Then you ran in the room and locked the door without answering any questions and making crazy statements like I'm some niggah you dealing with on the street. What was I supposed to do? Did you expect me to knock the door down and tear the trim off the hinges?"

All she could say was, "I'm so sorry Ervin, will you ever forgive me."

I said, "We have to seek counseling if we intend to stay married."

She seemed like she hadn't gotten much sleep at all last night and I didn't want to put any more stress on her and the baby. I went to pick her up and she said quietly, "I can walk."

"Ok Wynona, you need to be in bed so you can rest. I don't know where you stayed last night or if you got any rest but this couch is not a good place for you to be right now." I helped her down the hallway. She looked like she was ready to pop any moment. I pulled her slippers off and put her in the bed. As I turned to walk out the room Wynona said again, "Ervin, I didn't mean to hurt you; I just wanted to know where you were last night, I really am sorry." She started crying so I went back over to the bed. I was in no mood to hold her so I sat on the side of the bed assuring her that things would be ok. I told her to stop making herself upset it wasn't doing her or the baby any good. She put her hand on my back; I got up and started to do things in the room. She just looked at me and said, "I'm sorry I scratched your back like I did."

I looked back at her and didn't believe a damn word she was saying. It was ok, Crystal had taken care of me.

"Ervin, I was so worried that I called your Grandparents."

I dropped my head. On top of everything else I have to call them now and let them know I'm ok. "Don't worry about it; I'll take care of it. Get some rest."

She said, "We can do this baby, let's start again right after I have the baby.

I called Grandpa the next morning, "Hey Grandpa."

"How are you son? "Where you been, you know your wife been looking for you."

"I know Grandpa, I've taken care of things."

"Oh, ok! She was crying and going on saying she didn't know where you were at."

I chuckled, "Yeah she was a little upset; we got in an argument."

"Your grandmother wants you to come move some furniture for her; you know my back won't let me do that sort of thing anymore."

"Tell her I'll get over there one day next week; I promise."

The next morning around 5am Wynona's water broke. I thought I was dreaming that I was sleeping in a puddle of water. She was shaking me telling me it was time. I was like, "Time for what"! Then it dawned on me, "Oh shit it's that time!" I jumped out the bed rushing around trying to put my pants and shirt on. She told me to calm down it was going to be ok. I went and got Angel and Willow dressed and got the baby bag and we headed for the car. I put Angel in her booster seat and strapped Willow in her car seat, then I jumped in and was ready to go. That's when I noticed Wynona wasn't in the car. I went back in the house to find her slowly coming up the hall way. I asked was she ok. She started to get short of breath and said, "This baby is coming rather quickly."

We got in the car and headed to the hospital; every few minutes she would holler out in pain. I tried to look at her and the road as I drove. I said a silent prayer that her and the baby would be ok. Her eyes were swollen from crying; I hope no one really noticed. By the time we got to the hospital her labor pains were now 4 minutes apart. I got a wheel chair and wheeled her to the desk; I was so nervous. A nurse came and took her to labor and delivery; they told me I could meet them once I had finished with the paper work. As I stood there looking around, it hit me that I was about to become a father once again. This day would change my life forever; I had mixed emotions. We had just been fighting 24 hours prior to our son being born; I pray we didn't cause him to come to early.

She gave birth to a beautiful baby boy; I was hesitant at first, he looked like me but I still thought, "Was he really mine." He weighed 9 pounds even and was long, 23 inches. My Grandparents came to the hospital to see their first great grandson. Grandma took the baby first, as before. She looked at the baby then at me and back at the baby. She held him close but she didn't say anything. I guess she didn't think he was cute. When Willow was born she said now this is a Wyatt. I was so proud of my son but she just sat in silence. Then my Grandpa said, "Let me see my great grandson." Grandpa said, "You is mighty dark little fellow to be in our family." ("Tell it Pops, teeeell it.") I chuckled, "Grandpa the baby was just born, he hadn't got his color yet. ("And you ain't got yo damn eyes yet foo.") Wynona said it was time to feed the baby so I handed the baby to her. She looked nervous all of a sudden. I chalked it up to her just having a baby boy.

Mrs. Cary came up to visit as well, she held the baby as I walked my Grandparents to the elevator. My Grandpa and I walked ahead of Grandma. He asked, "Are you having a paternity test done son."

I said, "For what, I know he's mine."

My Grandpa leaned in close as if not to let Grandma hear him. "I don't think this is your seed. He don't look like you and he certainly doesn't look like his mom. I'm just telling you to be sure, don't be no damn fool."

I looked back at Grandma, I knew she heard what he said. She had this look on her face like check it out.

I went back to the room and I could hear Mrs. Cary and Wynona arguing, she said, "You better not let him down anymore, just walk away." I walked in the room and both women stopped talking. Mrs. Cary said, "Ervin, your son is so cute I bet you can't wait to take him home." I nodded my head in agreement but my mind was really on what Mrs. Cary was saying to Wynona just before I walked in. What the hell is really going on! (Ok fool, when are you going to listen to me? Will you take the wool off your eyes and see the obvious, damn!" I...)

My son was nothing like Willow, he cried most of the day not letting me get any rest. My mom didn't make it to the hospital to see her grandson; she called and said she was going to come by and see him.

A few weeks after bringing the baby home things seemed to be going well, we were a happy family. All of my fears were erased. Until one day I came home from work, the house was a mess, the two girls were sitting at the table eating and my son was in the crib crying. I asked my oldest daughter, Angel, where was her mother? She said her mom left with Mike. I was enraged! What the fuck is she thinking about leaving my damn children in the house by themselves? It was a good thing I was off the next two days. I was livid about what took place. I got the house in order and put the children to bed then I waited and waited for her to come in the door.

By the time she came home it was 4am in the morning. I asked her where the hell she had been and she said she was helping a friend who was having some trouble. I asked her what the hell was she thinking leaving the children in the house alone? She explained that her cousin assured her she was going to come to the house. I asked her what she was doing leaving with Mike.

Wynona asked, "Who said I left with a Mike?"

"Angel told me you left with Mike."

"Angel's a damn liar."

I asked Wynona was she happy in the marriage? She said she was happy but I knew in my heart it was a lie like everything else. I could feel myself coming unglued. My children were my world and there was no way I could leave them. I grew up without my dad and I would be damned if I was going to leave my children. I had to hang in there for the sake of them.

After a few weeks things didn't seem to get any better. Once again my Grandparents were a saving grace; as they did when Willow was born; they wanted Michael to be christened as well. As usual Grandma took care of all the arrangements. Wynona flat out said she wouldn't come this time; she felt it was a waste of time. I didn't see it that way and I wanted each of my children to be blessed by christening. Michael was almost two months old and everything was set for Sunday.

On the big day the girls were in pretty dresses and tights and we were on our way to my Grandparents' house for the traditional dressing of the baby. I took lil Michael up stairs so his great grandmother could change his clothes. As she undressed him she noticed he had the same two cherries like his two sisters on the same thigh. Grandma said she never seen three babies have the same birth mark. I thought of Wynona's body and she didn't have no cherries on her thigh. An alarm went off inside my head; how did all three children have the same birth mark.

("Don't worry it's just the idiot alert. Ok folks, nothing to see here let's break it up.") Grandma said, "Well don't concern yourself with it today, for today is anther special day in our family." She asked why I didn't name my son after me and I explained how Wynona said she wanted our son to be named by her favorite grandfather whose name was Michael; Grandma shook her head.

We all headed to the church; no one asked where Wynona was this time. When we arrived our family and friends were there and again my mom's friend Mike was there; he was just grinning. He said he was glad to be a grandfather; I just shook his hand and kept going. He talked to my grandmother as she held the baby. He told her the baby didn't look anything like me or Wynona. Grandma said she told him babies never look like anyone until they're at least six months old. I couldn't figure out for the life of me why he was there and my mother wasn't; it made me mad as shit. My Grandparents invited everyone over to the house for a Sunday evening feast. There I was with all three children by myself. Not only was it embarrassing, I couldn't understand how you can call yourself a mother and not be at your own child's christening. I was tired of covering and making excuses for Wynona. I knew in my heart I wouldn't ever leave my children but I was getting tired of how she treated me and our children.

The week before Wynona was going back to work. I had stepped out for a few minutes to go to the store. When I drove back up to the house I could hear someone arguing with Wynona. I opened the door, it was my mom.

She said, "You can't change a whore into a house wife." Wynona told my mom to kiss her ass. I asked what was all the arguing for. Her and my mom stood there glaring at each other.

I said, "Ok is someone going to tell me what's going on in here."

Wynona said, "Your mom is a bitch and I don't want her in my damn house anymore."

"Your wife is a big ass liar and I don't have to come over here; I have a house and for your information, this ain't your damn house it's Ervin's Ok bitch!"

"Ok ladies since neither of you are making since as to why you two are beefing, can you just go home mom. I appreciate you coming over to see your grandson."

"What damn grandson, that ain't none of mine!"

Wynona came over to my mom and tried to slap her, I was like are these two getting ready to go to blows. ("You got to be the dumbest niggah in the world. Move out the way and let these two bitches fight.")

"Bitch you might hit me and get away with it but what you don't understand is what you do in the dark will come out in the light one day."

"Mom please just leave, I'm sorry I'll take care of Wynona."

After my mom left I looked at Wynona, I said, "Why would my mom be saying all these ugly things about you if she didn't have a reason to. ("Wha, wha, what! Is you tryin to wake up chief nowannasee?")

"Ervin your mother is delusional, she seems to think because she has seen me several times in the club, which you already know about, that Michael isn't yours."

"Well is there any truth in what she's saying Wynona."

She said flat out, "Honey I know this is your son without a doubt, I never slept with anyone else." I found that very hard to believe as I still remember the incident where she stayed out all night long with her ex; who's to say she hadn't been doing that all along. ("Well I be damn, your dumb ass is finally waken up.") There was so many things on my mind I didn't know what to believe anymore. I just knew I loved my son. ("Shit, spoke too soon.")

She went right back to work after her six week checkup. I now had two babies to handle and the up keep of the house.

Not long after my son was born my brother came to visit. Don seemed unhappy; I asked what was wrong. He said he didn't want to be in a relationship with Jenny anymore. He said the more he gave her the more she wanted. Don said he was working long hours and could not get enough sleep. Jenny complained that it was his fault why Brianna was deaf.

I explained to my brother that some babies are born this way and it's no one's fault. He said well Jenny was sure trying to make him pay for it being his fault. I shook my head; this bitch was never going to change. That's why I wished a few years ago she had just left him alone. Don picked up his nephew and said, "Damn, Willow and

Michael are different as night and day." ("Everybody but yo ignant ass can see HE AIN'T YOURS NIGGAH!")

I asked my brother what he meant. He said Willow was chestnut brown with light colored eyes and had my clef chin. As for Michael he had dark eyes and was dark as Wynona and had no clef chin. Don said he don't look like neither one of you guys. I stood there shocked, how could he see all of this and the baby was just two months old. ("CUZZ DA LIL NIGGAH AIN'T YOURS YOU STUPID ASS BLIND MUTHAFUKA! You know what, I'm goin on vacation. Dis punk ass niggah dun got on my last nerve.") Don said well he my nephew anyway.

Don visited for a few more hours; after he left I picked my son up and held him. I sat in the chair: are you mine or are you Mike's son? Hell it could even be someone else's. I needed to have a test done. My Grandma called and said my Grandpa had been rushed to the hospital. I got the diaper bag together dressed everybody and headed toward the hospital.

As I drove up to the hospital I called Wynona and told her to please come over to the hospital after work, my Grandpa had taken sick. I went in the waiting room and found my Grandma sitting in the chair crying. "Grandma what's wrong?" "Your granddaddy has had a heart attack." I was like Fuck, can anything else happen!

I put Willow and her doll in the chair, I set the car seat down; Michael was fast asleep for a change. I sat in the chair next to Grandma and wrapped my arms around her. I told her he would be ok, he said he had been tired lately but I didn't know he was this sick. I asked her had she called my mom. She said she did but got no answer. There was no telling where her nasty ass was or what she was up to.

We sat there for what seemed like hours. Willow was now asleep and Michael was awake. I fed and changed his diaper but he was being noisy. He was looking around; Grandma said he was very alert like I used to be. I smiled, "Grandma you remember me way back then."

"Sure I do! I remember it like it was yesterday. You were a good baby, never gave us an ounce of trouble. On the other hand that Don gave me a run for my money. I thought he would never stop hollering."

I knew what she was talking about, Michael was being good for the moment but he could holler as well. I was doing everything I could to keep her mind off what was going on in the back.

I handed the baby to my Grandma and went to the front desk to ask about my Grandpa. I was told someone would come out shortly to talk to us.

"What did they say son?" "Someone will be out shortly."

My Grandpa died that afternoon. I had to stay strong; I had to be there for my Grandma and my mom. It hurt like hell cause I didn't get to see him before he passed away. I will take all the lessons he taught me and be strong for my family.

Grandma buried Grandpa in his marine uniform; she said that's what he wanted. Everything was sweet; she had his funeral at Sweeney's House of Rest. I saw friends there I hadn't seen in years. I thought I had even seen Crystal. People said my grandfather was a good man and helped everybody at some point in their lives. Reverend Still said he was going to remember that my grandfather had love for all his brothers and sisters. He said my grandfather often talked about his grandsons. He told Don and I to hold our heads up and continue to raise our families like he wanted us to. I took my grandfather death so hard. The realization that he wasn't going to get to know my son bothered me greatly. My mom and Don never even shed a tear. My Grandma and I both were overcome with emotion. I knew she would miss him; they had been together over 55 years. They had made plans and were going to go on a cruise to celebrate there 55 years together. Grandpa talked so much about this trip and was looking forward to getting on board and enjoying himself. Now it's only a memory of the joy and love he shared with his family.

It seems like time just flew by, one minute my children were babies and the next thing I remember they're in grade school. Wynona and I fought all the time about how the children should be raised. I felt because I gave them the most guidance I would discipline the children. She always wanted the children to take the easy way out of things. I wanted them to understand you can't have everything you want without someone working hard enough to get it.

As the children grew the requests for things just got bigger and bigger, and they wanted to do so many things. If I could have gotten just one thing I wanted I would have been good. These rascals wanted it all. To keep from going bankrupt I had to slow them down so I did my best to instill in them the value of working for whatever they wanted, how to manage money and set aside what they could in order to eventually get what they wanted.

I made up a list of chores for each of them to do for every day of the week. For every item that was completed on the list correctly they got a dollar. I refused to let them think they could keep dirty rooms or leave there things lying around like their mother did or my mom. They had to earn play time but I also let them know they couldn't get anywhere without proper education so for every "A" or "B" grade they got $5, and they had study time for at least two hours every day. I even devoted time away from my sleep to get up and go over homework with them.

When the children would ask Wynona for help she would tell them to ask me; she didn't have time. The children would tell me that their mother would leave them and go out all the time. She would come in from work and change her clothes and head right back out. She wouldn't even check on them to see if they needed anything. I just shook my head; I had always been there so I just played the role of the mother and father.

Looking back, I watched Willow and Michael take their first steps, I pulled their first tooth and I watched them go off on their first day at school. When they got sick at school they called me. They hardly ever called Wynona; she said it was best for them to call me since her job was so demanding. I never asked her for any of the money she made working for whoever. I remember one time Michael was going on a trip and I had forgotten to bring money home, I asked Wynona to give Michael money. She bit my head off and asked me was she made of money. I thought to myself, "What the hell, I never ask you to pay for anything." I pay all the bills, buy the food and pay for the children's clothes for the most part. There were a few times that she bought them something but when I looked at what she bought it didn't amount to anything worthwhile. Wynona was into buying shoes, pocket books, clothes and makeup for herself and of course smell good.

Angel's mother told her the basics about getting older but she still needed guidance on how to keep her body and clothes clean when it came to personal things like that.

I remember telling Wynona she needed to talk to Angel about her hygiene. She would hoot and holler saying she would take care of it when she came in from work. Well low and behold she never had the conversation with her so I took it upon myself to sit Angel down and tell her the facts of life and the personal things she needed to know. Angel hugged my neck and said I was the best. I didn't know what to think; Wynona had always been distant when it came to her oldest daughter.

Angel became rebellious and I had to go to the school several times because she would either get into it with the teacher or another student. Angel went so far as to go to school with her mother's tight jeans on, a small shirt and didn't wear a jacket. She was sent to the principal's office for flirting with some of the students in class. I was called to come get her since she didn't want to obey the rules.

When we got in the car I asked her what she wanted to do after finishing high school. She said she wanted to be an administrative assistant for a big company. I chose my words wisely and said that wouldn't happen if she continued to do whatever it is she wanted to do instead of following the school rules. I told her there were always consequences to the things you do. I told her she would be grounded for two weeks and she needed to tell her mother what she did to land herself in trouble. Angel hated talking to her mother and always complained to me that her mother wasn't right. Looking at it now Angel went through a phase where nothing was good to her; she hated life and hated her mother but she loved her brother and sister. She said the best thing that ever happened to her was when her mom gave her not one sister but a brother too.

When Willow was in the sixth grade she started her menstruation and instead of going to her mother she called her grandmother. And of course my Grandma called me; I was prepared. I now understood why they didn't go to their mom; she was never there for them. The children said she was always in a hurry or asleep and when they would try and ask her things she would cuss them out. Damn this shit was so familiar I was like when will this vicious cycle ever end. I was doing my best to break the mold.

Wynona and I were almost living like roommates; we slept in the same room when she would come in after being out late but that's it. The smell of booze and cigarettes was sickening and I would just turn over and say, "Ok lord, when will this shit end." I wanted so badly to be happy. Every now and again she would appease me with her sex but even that wasn't good anymore. I felt like she wasn't giving me her all. I'm in no way a punk but I just felt like soon and very soon my children were going to be grown and I was going to get up and walk straight out this heffa's life one day. I didn't even argue anymore, she wasn't worth the breath.

I made sure my children had what they needed and I made sure they grew up not being selfish, uncaring or even remotely like my mom or my wife.

Before I knew it, time had gone by and my children were just a few years away from becoming adults. I loved them to life but I was secretly preparing for the day this shit was going to end; meaning being married to a bitch that had no real feelings for me or her own children. It's hard to believe she actually carried each one for nine months.

Even though I hadn't seen her for a while I still thought of Crystal. There were even moments I wished for the phone to ring and in my own loneliness I knew it wouldn't happen. I wished her nothing but the best.

Turning 15 Michael wasted no time in asking me about getting his license. I guess he was beginning to get just as tired of his mother as I was. Now that Michael was old enough to actually get one, I decided to start taking him out, as I did with Willow, and show him the ropes. He was more exited then nervous and wanted to know everything. I laughed and told him to slow the brain down big fella. We went out to one of my favorite spots; High Mountain Church's huge parking lot that looked like it could pass for an airport runway. If he hit anything out here he would have to go way out of his way to do it and I was asleep when it happened.

I found a starting point and we stopped and got out. I took him around the car so he could check to make sure the lights and signals worked, and check the tires to make sure they were properly inflated. With all that done I had him get in, buckle up and adjust the mirrors. When he was finished I said, "Ok, now start the car." He turned the key and it fired right up. I told him to put his foot on the break and then on the gas. I just wanted to make sure he knew which was which. After that I told him to take the wheel and swing it back and forth so he would get a feel for how it worked with the car.

Now that all the kinks were out I told him to put his foot on the break, put it in drive and press on the gas. Why in the world did I say that? This boy hit the gas and we shot out like someone was chasing a getaway car. I yelled out,

"HIT THE BREAKS!" Why the hell did I say that shit? I couldn't get mad at him cause he did exactly what I said but damn. It's a good thing I had my seatbelt on cause I think I would've been on the hood at this point. After I retrieved my heart from the back seat and regained my composure, I calmly asked, "What the hell made you do that?" This lil niggah said that's what he saw them do in the movies. I said, "If you do that again, I'm gonna take this fist right here, and put it in that eye right there." He laughed at me and said, "I got it dad." Despite his initial epileptic fit starting out, Michael did well with everything I told him to do after that. With a little more training he shouldn't have any problem getting his license.

Because of my work schedule I didn't have a lot of time to spend with the children but when we did I made sure we had plenty of fun with whatever we did. Some of their favorite things to do early on was going to the park, shopping at the mall and eating out, but their favorite was going to the movies. They loved sitting in their own seat with a big bag of popcorn, candy and a drink. I took them to see Hook, Lion King, Toy Story, The Never ending Story II, Jurassic Park, The Mask and any other movie they wanted to see. My Willow was something else when it came to shopping though. She was a little deva already and knew what she wanted; I was really amazed at this girl because she actually had an eye for fashion. For a minute I thought about taking her shopping with me to pick out my stuff but that was a little too much.

My babies have grown up so fast and I wish I could've done more with them. All of this working and sleeping because I'm too tired and this crazy woman I call my wife who won't lift a hand to help with anything is driving me up the wall. Could it be this difficult for everybody or was it just me? I know things will change in time but damn, can a brotha get a little break somewhere?

Chapter 13

I wanted to go back to school so I could get another level of clearance on my job. I started school knowing I didn't have the full cooperation of Wynona but she said we needed the money so she told me it would be ok for me to go to school two mornings a week.

Once the children were of age Wynona decided that she had had enough of being a parent and got mad for no reason. She lost patience and decided she wanted to go back to school after me being in school for two semesters. She began accusing me of having affairs with classmates when all I was doing was receiving help from a study group. Every day she found a reason to argue.

I liked the work I did and got up every day wondering what will God have me to do today. After being married now for over 16 years I didn't feel like my life was being fulfilled. The past few years had been absolutely miserable for me. You did notice I said miserable right? I called Crystal one night to check on her as she had always been the one to check on me. She answered and her voice was so upbeat, I could tell she was happy. I made small talk then asked did she want to meet me for drinks on Friday night? She agreed to come. When I hung up I said to myself, "I don't know why I asked Crystal to meet me but a part of me felt at peace."

Friday couldn't come fast enough; I was glad to be going out and doing something different, I desperately needed some down time. Crystal was standing in front of the café, her smile was bright and she looked fantastic.

She said, "Hey Ervin how are you this evening?" I smiled, I was glad to see my friend. I hadn't seen her since that night she took care of my wounds and met Willow. Crystal and I were so close you would have thought we were dating. I asked her had she found any one to date yet. She told me she wasn't looking, she was still waiting on God to bring her husband to her. I felt sorry that she didn't have someone in her life, she deserved to be happy. We did what we normally did, engage in conversation and enjoy each other's company. We both were content on having drinks and grabbing a bite to eat when we could. She looked at me with that stern look and piercing eyes and asked me how things were going at home. I told her they were just going. She asked had we gone to counseling. I explained that after the baby was born Wynona changed her mind and said we didn't need any help.

As we left the Café I told Crystal I felt so bad dragging her out here to eat and have drinks with me so I could simply vent. She said she was fine with it. I looked in her eyes and knew she loved me, and there wasn't a damn thing I could do. I made up in my mind I was going to let Crystal live her life and hopefully she could find a good suitor. I wasn't going to continue this charade as it was hurting me because I couldn't be with her and it seemed like she was satisfied with just a dinner or drinks. Although that was my thought, I knew she had to feel something more because if she didn't she wouldn't always be there for me like she is, and I didn't want to cause any further pain to her. Why do the right things always seem so hard to achieve?

What constitutes a happy marriage? Is making love to her on nights when it's cold, brushing her hair back from her eyes and telling her how much you adore her enough? I felt pain inside and I didn't like it. I thought as a man I was doing all the right things but inside I could feel myself slowly growing away from her.

Wynona had gone back to school and I again, dropped out for the sake of the children.

When I look at my wife now days I feel empty. What would make a man feel as I did; Was it the fact she never had time for me, was it college or another degree she was falling in love with. It hurt me to think I worked two jobs and went to school to make sure we had all the things she wanted but yet I was lonely feeling pain deep down inside. I tried to talk to her about how I felt but she didn't see what I felt. I continued to help her with each degree she pursued. As she increased in degrees I started to hear things I never expected to hear. She would say, "Why you don't get another job?" or "Why don't you try and make more money?" I was making over $60,000 at the nuclear plant and the correctional officer paid me nice. My children never wanted for anything; we had three cars, a big house and a boat but I couldn't get rid of this damn pain I was feeling.

How is it that you can walk around as if the world owes you something when I can remember the day you had less and felt more? What makes a woman change and turn into someone I hardly recognize? I'm ashamed to say I'm losing my love all because she's pushing me away. I pray that my children don't see it? I wonder does she even sense what she is doing. I'm a man with feelings but I feel broken.

That night I got to work and things went from bad to worse. It wasn't enough that I had to deal with a bitch for a wife; I also had to deal with the pressure on this fuckin job. Every day I had to witness another inmate being viciously abused by the guards for simple little things that didn't require the least bit of punishment that was being dished out on them. I found myself stuck in the middle of my co-workers and the inmates; they both were looking at me sideways because I wouldn't participate in beating someone for nothing, and I didn't report it to my superiors either. I got to the point I couldn't take it anymore so I decided to start recording some of the events I was witnessing. If I wasn't gonna join with the people I worked with then I needed to do something to stop them from continuing to violate the guys we were supposed to be protecting.

I found a spy shop and ordered a small camera that I could fit in my hat and planned out how I was gonna accomplish my mission. The part that hurt most was Kevin, I grew up with this dude and what I have planned to do was going to affect him directly because he was one of the ring leaders. I knew each man was supposedly here for something they done but the harsh treatment they were receiving was despicable. I didn't know who to turn to or what to say. I thought of turning a letter into the news but unless they had proof they weren't going to investigate or report anything. These men were already being punished for their crime so I had to stand firm on my belief that every man must be treated with love and respect regardless of what they have done and get the evidence to fight this inhumane treatment. I may lose my life for fighting this cause but someone had to step up.

Losing sleep over Wynona and my job was really getting to me and I had to find relief soon or I was gonna lose it. I put my shield and uniform in the locker and drug myself out of the detention center. Kevin was outside smoking as I left the building, he said, "What's wrong Ervin you look like you're sick or something." He grabbed the top of my shoulder and clamp down on it and said, "Weak men don't get shit, but the ones that wise up get everything; pussy, drugs, and money."

I looked up at him; I was at a loss for words once again. I shook his hand off my shoulder and headed for my car. As I got in the car my heart was beating wildly, "Why me lord, why do you keep putting all this on me? Don't I go through enough at home? Didn't I go through enough growing up? I can't take this much longer.

I was glad the weekend was over; it felt like I was drowning so I laid down. I felt helpless. I could hear the children asking questions, I could see me working but it was like I was in a whirlpool; I was drowning. The week went by in a blur and it was Friday again. I couldn't muster up the energy to go in to the detention center and I knew I was in no mood to watch anymore beatings so I called in and told my supervisor I wasn't coming in; I had a lot on my mind. Not wanting to hear any more of this woman's mouth I played as though I was going to work and left; I had to get away so I went to a bar.

Wow, I couldn't believe I was taking my first drink after all these years. I wanted the feeling I felt to disappear and the pain to go away. The first drink burned as it went down. I heard usher playing in the background saying sign those papers. The first three drinks went down smooth and fast. I did a quick survey of the place and there was only about five others there besides me. I called the bartender over to pour another drink and a gray haired white man walked over and sat down next to me. I grinned and raised my glass to him; he nodded his head.

He said, "You put those first three down like they were water. You planning on taking the easy way out?"

"The easy way sounds really good right about now." I swallowed my drink and asked for another. I said, "You want to hear a fucked up story?"

He said, "Hell why not, I'm just sitting here nursing my scotch."

"My wife is a real bitch, I should have known this before I married her but I was just too damn blind to see. ("Fuckin deaf too! Don't forget to tell that part.") Will you shut up!

The man said, "I didn't say anything to you."

Oh, I said that out loud, "I'm sorry. I thought I heard someone else."

"Yeah, I know what you mean, I used to have one talking to me at one time too."

I just looked at him for a second not sure if he was talking about the same thing I was or not.

He asked, "What makes her a bitch son?"

"Who, oh you mean my wife. Well for starters she doesn't know how to give me respect. She always leaves me hanging to do every damn thing. When I say everything I mean everything! This drink is really damn good, another please." I smiled at the bartender.

"Well everyone has a little bitch in them every now and then."

"That's true but this is a 24/7 bitch here and if she ain't careful I'm gonna end up knocking her damn teeth out her mouth if she don't get her act together. ("Shiiit, he don't know you like I do.")

The guy chuckled; I just kept ginning. I was starting to feel like the incredible hulk and was getting hot inside; damn I was ready to fuck up some shit. ("No, that's just you getting fucked up stupid ass.") "Here's another one for ya; I got this other problem that's just as bad."

"What's that my man?"

"My damn job, I work at a detention center. They underestimate me as a man and think because I don't beat the inmates like many of the officers do for no reason that

I'm weak. Those men are already being punished for a crime so what's the difference between them and the officers committing crimes against the inmates? We're supposed to be protecting them. I know you don't care to hear this but there's some heavy shit going down and I'm at the point of exposing their grimy asses and leaving that fucking job; they're so dam disrespectful."

"Hold on, what kind of stuff are they doing?"

I waved him off, "Don't worry about it, I got it all under control. Now getting back to why I'm sitting on this bar stool and not at home with my family. I'm thinking about getting a divorce."

"Well friend let me tell you something, if you don't stand up for what's right you'll fall for anything. What's your name bud?"

"Oh, just call me EW."

"It was nice to talk to you. If you need to talk to someone again you can reach me here." He slid his business card to me and walked off. It said he was with Channel 11 news as an investigative reporter. I put the card in my pocket and went back to my drink.

That was the first time the word divorce entered my mind. I felt sick and asked for another drink. Before I knew it ole boy behind the bar said "No more drinks for you pal." I tried to grin at him, like hell I was ok but I knew I was baked as they say. I tried to stand up only to fall back on my seat. I tried again to stand and steady myself but I had no control. I was pissy drunk so I sat back down. I turned and looked to the right, no one was there. Then I looked to my left and saw a shadow say, "I'll make sure you get home but you must make better choices because the next time you may not be so lucky."

Here I was a man lost and spiritually hurting, how did it all come to this. I don't ever remember getting up from the chair, being in my car or going home. I just knew I looked up and a bright light appeared. I opened one eye to see I was sitting in front of my nicely built home, a place that I had so often enjoyed coming home to. I closed my eyes again to adjust my mind and my head was spinning. I now felt embarrassed by my actions. I didn't want my children to see me in this state of mind. I cried out to God and said if he got me in the house I wouldn't do this ever again.

I opened the door only to be met with a voice saying, "Where in the hell have you been! Who is she! Your ass got to go."

"Now remember, this is the first time in years that I decided to go get a drink and it was because of your ass I went in the first place." How quickly people forget the damage they cause when they feel threatened.

I waved her off and headed towards the bedroom fast as I could, I felt my body about to spew out this foul awful drink all over the place. As I was headed towards the door a flash went through my mind telling me to turn around and spew it on her. I slammed the door shut and could still hear her screaming, "I called your damn job looking for you and your ass wasn't there, where the hell were you? I know you hear me." I sat down on the cold floor just in time to flip the seat up and let the sick warm liquid come up and out, it was so wonderful hugging that toilet. I now understood what Bill Cornsby meant when he said the joke about hugging your girlfriend on the cold floor. At least she didn't talk back or make me feel less than a man, she actually was a comfort. I sat on the floor and sang my song like many before me for what seemed like hours. I dragged myself up and got in the shower. I let the water beat hard against my skin. I needed to revive myself, but how could I, I felt like a failure. Where did this come from, how did it all start! I cried in the shower because I couldn't understand how I had ever reached this low point in my life. What did I do to deserve this? I felt like my life was spiraling out of control. Whoever said a man doesn't cry ain't a real fuckin' man and I'm not afraid to say I cried that night; I had no real answers why I felt so much pain. It was like I was almost non-existent. How do I conquer this?

What makes a man almost lose his sole only to gain it back again, it's his decision to let go and allow God to reign supreme in him. My focus can't be compared to another man for he knows not the pain that I've had to endure.

After working at the nuclear plant for seventeen years and a corrections officer on the weekends, I now had to consume the household duties from washing dishes, clothes and cooking; the only thing Wynona was good for was sitting her loud ass on the couch fussing at what I wasn't doing right! She became very rude and arrogant. I asked several times why she had stopped helping me take care of the family and for the most part she ignored me. Shit doesn't last always and you know God had something down the road for me. My entire motivation to stay in a marriage 18 years was my children, they were my main focus. I worked out at the gym as much as possible and hated going home but the love of my three children always drew me back home. I would lay in bed and think how she would act a fool. In my mind I would say, my day is coming; I wasn't going to hoot and holler, I just kept saying my day was coming and knew God had another plan for my future. I would tell my friend Ed all the time I couldn't wait for my 18 year sentence to be over.

That lady, my wife, I had known for the past 18 years of my life felt and looked like a stranger to me. I would come in and walk over to her, try to kiss her and she would move her face. The first time she did that shit it stung, so I felt maybe it was just me. I tried the next day, the reaction was the same. After a while it was like a switch, she would just turn on and off when she wanted to. After a period of time I just stop trying. Certain things she did started to turn me off. I wasn't going to cheat on her and the thought never crossed my mind but other men would have jumped to cheat just because she was acting like an ass. Unlike other men I never had a desire to go outside my marriage, I felt like this was it and I was going to be married forever. What a joke, and it was played on me. You laughin but that shit ain't funny yo.

Chapter 14

So at what point did I really see the glue come undone. It's ok to see a woman do certain things and you don't say anything but then she takes it a little too far. She had reached a point where she started spending money and not telling me until after it was done. It wasn't that it really mattered but we still had a house, three children and a mortgage to maintain. And I know I wasn't slack in doing my part.

Wynona was becoming selfish in her own way and she didn't want to talk or consult me about the simplest of things anymore. It was like the more degrees she went after the more she made me feel being married to me wasn't for her anymore. I wanted to make love, keep a happy home, and have my family close; this felt like a nightmare that just wouldn't quit. Just like my job, she was becoming an adversary in my home and she wanted to compete with me in everything. She couldn't understand why I had such report with the children. I would say I was confused, shocked even.

I was very skeptical about whether she would have more children after observing the way she treated our oldest daughter. We did eventually have two more children but she always wanted someone else to keep them. What kind of mother has children and leaves them for someone else to raise? She never really acted like children were a priority. I really thought to myself the only reason the children were here is because I wanted them. She made me feel like she really didn't want them but Willow and Michael were my pride and joy. Wynona always had a problem with how I chose to raise the children.

I wanted an open relationship with my children and I wanted them to be able to come and tell me anything or ask any question. I would always say no question was too dumb to ask. If they wanted something I just didn't give it to them, I would teach them the value of money and we would plan how we were going to get whatever it was they wanted. Their mother had no understanding of our relationship and she became enraged because the children would talk to me rather than her.

Wynona became angry when she realized she couldn't control my emotions, thoughts or ideas; that bothered her. She would attempt to throw up certain things in my face like, "Well, I'm five years older than you" and I'm saying to myself what the hell does a number have to do with the mentality of the persons thoughts, ideas and emotions. Someone would ask why did I stay in the marriage as long as I did and I would simply say my children.

I grew up without a father in a very dysfunctional family and I wanted my children to know who their father was. I wanted to raise my children and let them know I would always be there for them. I'm so grateful having the ability to watch them grow up to be respectable young men and women. They are a lot like me in a since; they love computers, movies and video games. My children and I are still very close; even my stepdaughter Angel who moved away from her mom because she no longer wanted her to control what she did and how she did it.

After all this time Michael finally went down and got his driver's license. During my off time between jobs we drove around for months so he could be comfortable driving. I was so proud of him. Willow and I would ride around with him; she said Michael was going to be her ride to the mall. He chuckled and said Willow was going to have to pay him. I sat and listened to them plan how they were going to do things together. They're extremely close and he usually won't move unless she does. I had given Michael permission to drive the spare car we had at the house. I know Wynona wasn't happy that Michael was going to be driving but I really wasn't concerned about her being mad cause she stays mad all the time. He had earned my trust and the privilege to drive so that's that. It was going to be less stress on me picking them up from the library and taken them to buy things at the mall. Michael and I had a long talk about what to do and how not to be having a conversation on the phone or not paying attention to the road while he was driving.

I was close to finishing my mission at the corrections facility and had compiled tons of evidence to prove any abuse of authority or rights violations case against many of the officers. I took the business card I got from the guy at the bar and called the number. The guy eventually answered and said, "Hello Doug Hutchens with news channel 11, how can I help you?"

I said, "Hi, this is EW, do you remember talking to me at the bar? You gave me your card and told me to call if I needed to talk again."

"Sure I remember, what can I do for you?"

"I have information and evidence of serious violations being committed by officers on my job that I'd like you to take a look at. If you have time I can meet you today and drop the package off."

"Sounds great, how about 4:30pm at the same bar?"

"Ok, I'll see you there."

I had just retrieved the last few documents I needed from the job when I got a call that Michael had been in an accident; he had only had his driver's license for about three months. I tried to call Wynona on the phone but it kept going straight to voice mail. I picked up Willow and headed to the hospital. She said she hoped it wasn't real serious, she was crying and said she was supposed to go with him to the Library but she hadn't finished her hair yet but he didn't want to wait. I told her to calm down and let's just pray for the best.

On the way to the hospital I called Wynona again several times, no answer. It had dawned on me that I had never actually gone to her job before. I could run by there but no I had to go to the hospital first, but maybe they could get a message to her. I called and the receptionist answered, "Thank you for calling Twin Towers how may I help you?"

"Wynona Wyatt please."

"Sir, there is no one here by that name."

"Ma'am, she's worked there for several years now, could you check again please, it's an emergency."

"Sure, what's the name again please?"

"Wynona Wyatt."

"I'm sorry sir, we don't have anyone here by that name and according to my records there has never been anyone here by that name. Will that be all?"

"Yes, thank you."

I wasn't completely sure if I heard what I just heard but I couldn't deal with it at that time; I had to find out if my son was ok. Willow looked like she wanted to ask me something but I think she sensed that this wasn't a good time. I was supposed to meet Doug Hutchens at news channel 11 after getting the package together so I placed a quick call to let him know I would have to call him after I got things under control with Michael to drop it off.

After getting to the hospital I was told that Michael's car was hit by someone said to be fleeing from a bank robbery scene and the getaway car struck his car and it flipped over at the corner of LaSalle and Morris. I wondered just what the hell Michael was doing on that street; it was nowhere near the library. I told the nurse who I was and she said it would be a few moments before I could go back to see him. She said the doctors were still assessing his injuries. I dialed my Grandma's number and told her where I was. I told her I had tried to reach Wynona but couldn't. She assured me that she would try the number as well and asked if I needed her to come over to the hospital. I told her Willow and I were here and she could stay at home; I would keep her updated on his progress.

After pacing the floor for an hour the Dr. finally came out and told us that Michael had ruptured his spline and had internal bleeding, and that he needed a blood transfusion at some point because he had lost a lot of blood. The doctor said he gave Michael something to keep him comfortable and that we could go back to see him now. I told Willow to come on, she said, "No dad you go. I don't think I'm in any shape to see my brother laying in a hospital bed. I'm going to keep trying to reach mom at work."

"Ok baby, good idea."

I looked at my son laying in that bed and my heart broke; I had to fight back the tears. I touched his face, he opened his eyes and said, "Hey dad, I'm sorry, I didn't mean to get in a wreck; it wasn't my fault."

"No son, shhhhhhh, rest. We'll work out all the details later. I do need to ask what you were doing on that side of town though. Who do you know over there?

Michael turned his face from me so I asked again, "Son, what were you doing on that side of town, that's a bad area; nothing is over there but pimps, whores and bars."

"Dad please don't make me tell you."

"Tell me what son?" My heart was starting to beat wildly; was he trying to get him some pussy, what!

"Dad if I tell you…you have to promise me you won't get mad at me."

"I won't son I'm just concerned about you that's all. I told you we'll work everything else out."

"Dad, its mom."

"What, what about your mom?"

Michael hesitated, "I was following her."

"Following her! To where son and why did you need to follow your mom; did she ask you to?"

"No dad listen, Willow and I have been watching mom leave the house with some man after you go to work for years. I told Willow when I got old enough to drive I was going to follow her to see where they go so I could tell you. That's why I was always wanting you to teach me how to drive so I could get my license. When you let me start driving the spare car was when I started following her. When they leave they go to this damn bar called Peeping Tom Bar on that side of town where I had the accident. I wanted to see what she does in the bar ok! I'll take my punishment dad; I didn't mean to get in a wreck."

My mind went crazy, hell this was the bar my damn mom hung out in; what the hell was going on now. The bar had changed names a dozen times but still it was a nasty place to be found in.

Michael saw the look on my face and started crying, "Dad I'm so sorry please forgive me, I know you told us not to lie to you but it hurt like hell to see mom always leave with this man and lying to you about going to work. I just had to know dad, for real I just had to know. When I was turning the corner up the street from the bar I started hearing police sirens so I turned my head to see and from out of nowhere this car was coming at me fast; there was nothing I could do. The last thing I remember was getting hit and the car going airborne; I blanked out."

"Ok son you rest now. I'll be back in a little while ok? I'm gonna ask Willow to come sit with you till I get back."

"Dad, are you mad at me?"

I touched his face and said, "No son, I could never be mad at you." I walked out of the room I told Willow to go sit with her brother; I had to leave but I would return as soon as I could. Willow said, "But dad I can't…"

Before she could finish I said, "Willow please go sit with your brother until I come back."

Willow stood up and said, "Is everything ok dad?"

"I'll explain everything when I return, just go do what I told you. Call me on my cell immediately if you need me or his progress changes. Call your grandmother and ask her to please come over to the hospital; she'll be glad to sit with you until I come back. Just tell her I'll explain everything once I come back." One thing about Mrs. Cary she was a good person. Her and Wynona had their issues but for the most part I stayed out of it.

Running to the car my mind was ablaze; I was like what the hell is really going on. Michael in the hospital, Wynona is nowhere to be found and he said he saw her going into that damn bar. The adrenaline in me was pumping so strong it felt like my whole body was about to explode. I got in the car and noticed an envelope placed under the wiper blade. I got out, snatched it off and threw it in the seat then drove off. It took me 15 minutes to reach the bar on Morris and LaSalle. I tried to steady my hands on the steering wheel, "Ok lord, I don't know what's going on but please don't let Wynona be in this bar." The bar was now called Peeping Tom Bar, what kinda damn name is that. I got out and headed toward the door. Upon opening the door the place reeked of booze and god knows whatever else. I waited for a second to let my eyes adjust so I could see; it was kinda dark. I walked to the left making a survey of the place; there were a few people huddled in the corner talking and drinking. I walked further in the bar; there was a few people sitting at the bar ordering drinks. From what I gathered they looked like normal people who just wanted to get there drink on. Maybe Michael made a mistake, then I heard a very formerly laugh coming from deep in the back corner past the dance floor. I followed the noise and as I got closer my head and chest felt like it was going to explode. Just behind a wall I saw her on top of some man pumping hard as she could and laughing, saying, "Is it good to you Mike."

I stopped and just stared, the guy saw me first; Wynona was gone, she never saw me coming. I shouted at the top of my lungs, "BITCH what the fuck are you doing?" Wynona jumped in shock and got off of him. She said, "Ervin, what the hell are you doing here!" she tried to push her dress down. I said, "No bitch, the question is why Wynona! Why!" Mike stood up and said, "This little niggah is your husband. I remember his momma tricking off all her money on me baby. Now I'm spending his money." Ervin had a flash back, this was the Mike that was fucking my mom and now he was fucking Wynona too! ("Ooooooooh, yes, he's finally gonna give me SUPPA NIGGAH! Hahahahahahahahah") I grabbed my chest and collapsed to the floor. ("Mutha Fuck, can one of yaw step in an help a brotha whup some ass roun here?") I heard someone say call the ambulance. It took several minutes for me to come to; they gave me some smelling salt in the ambulance. I was asked a series of questions, I could hear them but I couldn't answer them. I heard someone say his blood pressure is too high; we got to get it down before we lose him. I could hear her voice saying, "Are you taking him to memorial." They said, "Yes." She said, "I will follow you." I could hear Mike's voice say, "Hurry back now we got unfinished business to attend to." Wynona had a nerve to giggle. If I could have got up off the stretcher I would have put my foot all up in her ass. This Bitch was crazier than I could ever have imagined. I laid there thinking about Michael, Willow, my dad, my Grandma, Don and my mom. I thought I was dying.

We reached the hospital, they rushed me in and I was given a battery of tests. I was told it could be a heart attack or stress, they wanted to do more tests. I reached in my pants pocket, the phone had been buzzing.

"Hello dad, they need to do a blood transfusion on Michael where are you."

I whispered, "I'm in the emergency room Willow."

"Where dad, where!"

I told her I was in the emergency room too; I must have been on the other side. The next thing I remember Willow was standing next to my bed, tears were streaming down her face.

"What happened dad, please tell me what happened? Did you get sick in the parking lot?"

I couldn't shake the cobwebs from my brain. "Where is mom dad, I still haven't been able to reach her." Mrs. Cary followed Willow, she stood back; I could vaguely hear her praying.

When she said those words the inferno began mounting again. I motioned for Willow to come closer, "Please don't ask about your damn mother." Willow looked like she didn't know what to do at that moment. She just looked at her grandmother and shook her head.

Then Wynona came into the room, she looked at Willow, then her mother, then at me. She shook her head and said, "It don't make no damn since how a grown ass man fake a heart attack to keep his ass from gettin whupped." Mrs. Cary walked over to Wynona and said, "Child, I don't know the entire story but you have lost your damn mind. Your husband needs you right now."

Willow was shaking her head no.

I said, "Wynona please don't do this right here, right now; this is not the time or place. We have two crisis' going on. Are you going to stay with me until I can get my head together?" With the straightest face you can imagine she said she had to go to work and walked off. Mrs. Cary grabbed her shoulder and spun her around; before she could say another word her mother slapped the shit out of her. Wynona grabbed her face in shock and stormed out the room. This is another joke, I'm asleep right? One day this bitch is gonna pay for what she's done to me if it's the last thing I do.

Because I was in no shape to be the donor for my son's transfusion, Willow stepped up like the Angel she is and told the doctor's that she would do it. Mrs. Cary told me to take care of myself and that she would be here to support me and the children. I remember they went off and I just lay there doing my best to relax and not worry about what my babies were going through right now. I had to get better for them and couldn't keep going on the way I was. They were already just as stressed and with facing their own medical procedure and surgery, they didn't need more stress worrying about me also.

A couple hours later Willow was by my bedside calling my name. I must have finally dosed off. I asked her how everything went. She had this strange look on her face and said, "Dad, I can't do it, I don't have the right blood type." I sat up a little and took a drink of water to wake myself up more, "What did you just say?"

"I said I can't do it cause I don't have the right blood type."

"How is…where's the doctor?" I sat up fully on the bed and waited for the doctor to arrive. Dr. Pathak came in with Willow and asked how I was doing. I told him I was fine and asked him to explain what was wrong with my daughter giving blood for her brother's transfusion. He said, "Because your daughter's blood type does not match your son's, it would be impossible for us to use her as the donor for your son. Because of your condition we wouldn't be able to use you as the donor either. Is there someone else we can contact that may be willing to provide us with the blood we need for your son?"

I looked at Willow and wondered how that could be as I thought of who else I could call to help. I asked Willow to have her grandmother call and see where Angel was. She said she already called Angel and that she should be there in a few minutes. She was talking to Grandma who said she was on her way.

I asked the doctor what was my son's blood type. He said he was a B–. I was startled when I heard that because my blood type was O+. Then I asked what was my daughter's blood type and he said it was A+. My head started spinning again and the doctor made me lay down. Willow came to my side and said, "What's wrong dad, why are you acting like this?" The doctor asked her to go to the waiting room for a few minutes and he would come see her shortly.

"Mr. Wyatt, I know this has been very trying for you today with you getting sick and your son being in an accident but I must ask you; are these your children or did you adopt them?"

My head kept spinning, when was this shit ever going to end. How is it that neither of my children have the same blood type? The Doctor was still talking, I felt like I was slipping away. I had to shake my head and try to clear the cobwebs. "I don't know what's going on Dr. Pathak but I'll get to the bottom of it, you can rest assured of that." I felt like I was losing control of this entire situation and Wynona had the nerve to just leave me at a time like this. I needed her here for, if nothing else, moral support. "If my daughter can't give her brother blood is there a way to call and see if we can get some from the next city?"

"We can do that but it's much better for the patient if there's a relative who is a match that is willing to provide blood. It's also our first policy to try and stay local because it's faster and we can get the blood cleared. It's not that we can't do that if it's flown in we just don't want to waste any more time."

Angel came in a few minutes later; she asked was I going to be ok. I told her I was going to be fine. She asked where her mother was. I said, "I can't talk about that right now, it's only going to cause me to get upset again and I don't want to have a heart attack. I need to stay calm right now Angel; my head is killing me."

She said, "Well I gave them blood to see if I was a match."

"Thank you Angel."

"I don't really see why Willow couldn't; we are all sisters and brothers."

"It's a long story Angel." I appreciated what she did for Michael but I knew we would need to find someone else or have blood brought in from somewhere else.

"Dad, both Grandmas are outside; do you want me to go out in the waiting room with Willow so Grandma can come in, she looks like a nervous wreck."

"Sure, that's fine. Hey Angel, thanks for coming over so fast."

"Dad, that's my brother over there and I would do anything for him, my sister or you; and mom, even though she gets on my nerves."

As my Grandma walked up and sat down, the Dr. came back in and said, "I have some good news." but hesitated because my Grandma was sitting there. I told him it was ok to talk in front of her.

He said, "The older sister is a perfect match so we can prep your son and get started right away."

"Thank God, so we can move forward.

"Yes we can."

I was so happy.

"I'll go and inform your daughter of the news and ask her to step back in so we can prep her as well." The Dr. left the room.

My Grandma said, "What does he mean Angel is a perfect match? Why not Willow or you?"

"Grandma it's a long story."

My Grandma gave me a blank stare like I'm not going anywhere please explain.

"I will explain Grandma, let me just make sure Angel understands everything first ok."

"Ok Ervin, don't think I'm gonna forget. I'll be right here waiting."

"Angel did the Dr. explain what will take place and what you need to do?"

She said, "Dad, I'm all for it. I'll see you in a little bit." She came over to the bed and whispered, "Get well dad, I need you." She kissed my forehead and walked off. That girl just doesn't know how much of an Angel she really is to me.

When she was out of listening range I looked at my Grandma and went into detail about what had taken place. My Grandma yelled out, "You did what! That nasty no good heffa. I will beat the living…"

"Grandma, Grandma please calm down; listen. Aaaaaa my head is hurting bad."

"Oh, Ervin baby, lay down."

I took her hand and said, "Grandma I just need you to stay calm for me until Michael is out of the woods."

"I will don't you worry. But Ervin, does that mean neither one of these children are yours?"

"Grandma I don't want to think about it right now, please. If it's true that these aren't my biological children, I will never treat them any differently; they didn't ask to come here. ("That's right gramma cause we gonna open a can of whup ass when we get out a here.") I'll continue to love them anyway, just like I do there sister Angel." I had to hold on; I won't break down in front of my Grandma. She had to endure a lot losing Grandpa, dealing with my mom acting like an ass all the time and to find out my wife has been cheated on me this entire time; and now these children are not mine. The funny thing about all of this is they sound and act like me.

Dr. Palek came in and said the blood transfusion went well. He said Michael was resting comfortably and Angel was having orange juice and cookies; she would be coming back up here in a few moments. Because of my present condition he recommended that I stay overnight so they could monitor me and make sure I didn't have a heart attack. I said ok and thanked him for everything. As he was about to walk off he looked back and said, "I hope everything turns out well for you and your family."

A few minutes later I was taken to my room in another wing of the hospital and was told that another Dr. would be in to see me shortly. I laid there confused by the days events. My Grandma had gone to get her some coffee. I figured this would be a good time to call my mom and ask her could she please come over to the hospital, that way my Grandma could go home if she chose to; which I already knew she wasn't going to leave until I did.

My heart was heavy and numb; I was losing all hope in myself. If there was a way for me to end my life I would but I knew God had something better for me so that wasn't an option; I was being tested. I loved my children more than life itself and I wasn't going to leave them now; they needed me.

I finally got around to calling my mom and asked her to please come over to the hospital. I told my mom everything that had happened. The whole time my head was pounding like someone took a brick and hit me and on top of that my chest was tight as hell, it felt like I was having a heart attack; it hurt bad. The Dr. came back in and said my son was out of the woods. He also recommended that I see the psychologist for a few minutes. I told him that would be fine.

As soon as the doctor was gone my mom started in on me about Wynona. She said. "I told you a long time ago you can't turn a hoe into a house wife."

Why did she go there? Something clicked inside of me and it just started coming out. ("IT'S ME NIGGA! IF YOU AIN'T HAD ENOUGH, I SHO HAVE!") I looked at my mom, raised up off the bed and my mouth started moving, "Hold on a minute bitch! After all that I just told you, that's all that's on your fuckin mind? Who the hell are you to talk about anybody? Do you fuckin remember all the shit you did to me growing up? No, you were drunk with your legs in the air most of the time. I have asked you to support me on several occasions and if my memory serves me correctly you fucked up each one of them times. Not only that, you kept my damn father from me and on top of everything else you took his money every month and spent all of it on yo fuckin ass and none on me. I can't count the number of days you left me and Don in that damn house starving. Do you remember that mom? Oh yeah, you were drunk with your legs in the air most of the time. Do you remember us going without clothes and toys? All you thought about back then was finding a way to get your ass wet and that's still all you fucking think about. It's a wonder your ass is still alive. I'm even fuckin surprised yo ass is even standing there right now. Don't look at me like that, hell I've kept this shit in long enough. You been doing this shit my whole life and you want to come in here and talk about my damn wife! WITH ALL THE SHIT I'M FACING RIGHT NOW, THAT'S ALL YOU GOT TO THINK ABOUT? REALLY! ("Aaaaaaa woooooooooooo, niggah please niggah please, somebody bring me da cape and my walkin stick. Supa nigga dun jumped all in dat ayass. Where da popcorn!")

"How dare you!"

"Why don't you dare to walk yo stank ass out of my face. I don't need you either. If you can't for once in your life do something good for me then get the fuck out! You can go

hang with your sister Wynona without hidin' it now."
("Wow, he did that on his own guys; I was finished.")

My mom took her pocketbook and stormed out the room. My head started to spin out of control again; I fell back and the door swung open again; to my surprise stood Dr. Crystal Foster. We both looked at each other in amazement. I didn't know who was more shocked, me or her. Dr. Foster gathered her composure, took the chair and moved it closer to the bed. "Mr. Wyatt what brings you here today?"

I thought I would choke. I sat there silent for a few moments as she looked at me; her eyes pleading for me to open up. I hesitated for a few more moments and then began to tell my story. I thought I was about to lose my mind. Actually it felt like I was having a heart attack only to find out I was suffering with an anxiety attack. Dr. Foster put me out of work until further notice. Since I wasn't a threat to myself or others she let me go home. I, a grown as man, sat there and cried like a baby. I told the woman I had loved for many years I was tired and didn't feel like I could take any more shit off of anyone including my mom and my wife. I had a hard time dealing with the stress and was put on medication. Of course she advised me that I seek counseling for the issues I was facing. I would become short of breath and my chest would tighten up, I really thought I was losing my mind. I continued to lay in bed waiting to be released from the hospital.

There was another knock on my door. I said, "Come in!" Everything came to a dead holt; I wasn't sure if I was dreaming or what but standing in the doorway before me was the man I needed and searched for so long, my dad. I raised up and before I could utter a word he came over to my bed and embraced me.

Still speechless he said, "This to will pass, you just have to become strong enough to leave the situation. Your children are old enough for you to walk away and be free now. Do it son before I have to end up burying you."

Something deep in me began to burn and the tears became uncontrollable. I looked up into his eyes and asked, "Dad…how did you know I was here?"

"My good friend the detective who has always kept up with you for me was here with his grandson. He saw you when you came in and said you looked like you were in bad shape. Once I heard I said now it's time for me to step in and come to your aide. I stepped in once before but you were so drunk I don't think you ever knew it was me who made sure you got home that night. I walked all the way back to the bar and got my car. I couldn't let you drive; if I did I knew it would be the last time because I believe you would've given up and died in a car wreck. You are and always will be my son. From here on out I'll make sure you never forget that."

I cried even more, my dad has been my guardian Angel all these years. "Thank you for coming dad, I truly need you right now."

"I know, just promise me you won't give up son."

"I won't dad, I promise. I'm going to fight through all the hurt and pain my mom and wife have caused me. The only joy I've had is my children, my Grandparents and my best friend, and to make matters worse the lady I have been in love with for years is the Doctor who treated me today, which just happens to be my best friend." I thought I would die.

"Son remember, if it's real love it stays around even if you're not ready for them. Maybe that's how God intended for it to be; everything had to come out and be released into the open. Just be patient son, you'll see. When you are better there's something else I need to discuss with you that's very important."

I was a little confused and concerned to hear him say that but I did as he asked and focused on getting myself better for now. The doctor came to see me just about every hour until it was time for me to be released. It seems I was a high risk for a heart attack because I held onto everything. I didn't know how or what to do to release all the pain that was building inside me; no one ever taught me about that part before.

In the waiting room before leaving the hospital, everyone I loved was there; my Grandma sat there looking up at me. I could see tears in her eyes. My mom sat in the corner with envy. My big brother got up and hugged me. Brianna was with him, she couldn't speak but when she seen me her face lit up like a light bulb. She had grown to be a beautiful young woman and looked just like her dad. She was definitely a daddy's girl. Don said when he left the house she would always tag along unless he was going to see one of his night walkers. My dad stood beside me proud that he had come to the hospital to see me. My Grandma asked where I was going now that I was being released. I hadn't really thought about it but I knew I had to at least face my wife and see my children.

Wednesday was a wake-up call for me to change my life; my children were now 16 and 17. I had to get out before I went crazy or lost my life. Wynona and I fussed about why she didn't stay at the hospital with me. She told me if I didn't like it I could get the fuck out. It finally dawned on me that this bitch was really trying to kill me so I calmed myself down and said, "You're right, I'll be leaving but this is far from over." I got choked up but I had to tell her what was on my mind and what happened at the hospital.

"You know, it's been a long hard road with you but to find out that I'm not the father of your two children was very disheartening to say the least. There was always something telling me to get away from you but I stayed because I thought it was the right thing to do. It hurt like hell to find out I had been living a lie being married to you.

Why didn't you just let me go in the Marines and leave me alone; why did you have to fake your life with me all these years? I know I may not get this right but I believe Mike is the father of those children. Will I ever treat them any different? No! I raised a set of children who aren't mine biologically but they are mine in spirit and there's nothing either of you can do to change that. At some point I'll sit down with them and disclose the damn truth."

I remember standing there with clinched fists; I was furious as I tried to keep my emotions together. My Willow touched my arm and told me to calm down; everything will be alright now. I think I would be dead if it wasn't for her and Grandma; they were always there at the right time.

Wynona looked like a rag to me now; she was no longer the beautiful bronze princess I met all those years ago. "My entire life I felt lost and didn't fit in but I made it work because at least I had Grandparents who I knew loved me. I now know the reason you and my mom got in that fight that day. She knew what you was doin with all those niggah's and threatened to tell if you didn't stop fuckin her man Mike. My mom is just as low down as you because she didn't tell me in the beginning. Neither one of you have a sole and you're both going to hell if you don't change your nasty ass ways. Don't ever contact me again for anything; I'll send you the divorce papers."

Wynona stood there embarrassed and in shock that I knew and tried to speak. I said very calmly, "Save the lies for the trash you've been with all these years. I no longer hear you."

Willow couldn't hold it any longer and just exploded on her mother. "Mom I have never once got in between you and dad but you're dead wrong. All these years I watched you parade around here like you were my mother but what you don't know is this; you'll never fit my dad's shoes. He's taught me more than you'll ever teach me; I can't stand being in the same fucking room with you. I knew something was up with you all those times I called that damn job and they said you didn't work there; you're a fuckin liar. I was too afraid to break my dad's heart but you seem to be real good at it. You're a whore and have always been a whore, and because of you Michael almost died! Have you ever wondered why your own damn daughter don't want to be bothered with your ass? Hell she knew as well and we both said it would come out one day; I just didn't think our brother would be the victim of your ungodly deeds."

Wynona raised her hand like she was gonna smack Willow.

Willow looked straight at her mom and said, "Mom, I promise you I'm not dad. If you hit me right now I'll stomp the shit out of you for what you've done to us."

("Now that's my fuckin girl! Why you can't be like her? Oh, you not her daddy. Oops!")

I think I was just as shocked as Wynona to hear those words but I allowed her to speak her mind. It was time we all released the anger that had built up over the years. I took my Willow's hand and we left her mom standing there by herself.

Later that night Angel showed up over to the house and came out on the deck with Willow and I. I kissed and hugged her then left the girls alone; they talked for more than an hour before they came into the house. As they went into the living room it looked like they had been crying. Angel said, "Mom I didn't come over her beause I feel sorry for you, I came to help bring some of these issues to a close. Although you might not like what I'm about to say, I'm gonna ask that you don't interrupt me until I'm finished. My brother's lying in the hospital because of your ungodly ways."

"I ain't got to listen to this."

I said, "Wynona, sit your ass down and listen to what she has to say. You been dishin' out shit for years, now it's time you hear it from someone else other than me."

"Fine Ervin, fine!"

"Angel started again, "I can remember as a child how you and Mike, the man that is supposed to be my father, would be in the bedroom fucking."

As soon as those words came out Wynona began to speak again and Willow jumped up and stepped in between her mother and me. I guess she didn't notice what was about to happen because she was focused on Angel but when she looked at me she could see all the years of rage coming from me at that moment and backed up.

Willow said in a soft voice, "Dad, I know but we have to get it all out and Angel and I need you to stay calm while we go through this ok." She touched my face and repeated the words, "I know dad." No matter how angry I got Willow was always able to calm me.

Angel looked at me and asked if it was alright to continue and I said, "Yes baby please go ahead. I'll be ok."

“Mom, you might think I was too young but I remember like yesterday Mike telling me to shut the fuck up because I walked in on you two. At the time I didn’t know what you were doing but as I grew older I knew how dirty you were. You never told me Mike was my dad, my grandmother told me Mike was my dad. I grew up hating you for the way you treated me or should I say didn’t treat me because you acted like you wanted nothing to do with me. My real dad (pointing at me) basically took care of me and my siblings; you were just a baby carrier. I couldn’t wait to be grown so I could get the fuck out. At one point I was goin down a very bad road but my dad talked to me and guided me through it; he kept me on track, not you. I knew I didn’t want to be anything like you; a liar and a nasty cheatin hoe. There were times I wanted to tell dad you didn’t have a job or you weren’t at that fake job you say you were at. I knew it would kill him. I understood why he worked as hard as he did, he wanted to provide a good home for us, and he did just that. He loved you and wanted you to have the best of everything but you did nothing but belittle him. To have a man like dad and treat him the way you do, I honestly think you’re crazy. Mom, I hope and pray you get your life together before you end up just like Grandma Molly fucking everybody. You don’t have to worry about throwing me out or cussing me out when I leave. The only time you're gonna ever see me again is when I come back to see my sister and brother graduate from high school."

The house was totally silent for several minutes. Willow and Angel were standing on each side of me with their arms around me; tears were just flowing down my face. ("Yeah niggah yeah, I tried to tell you but I won't be hard on you now, Shit!") "I just want to tell both of you how proud I am of you and that I love you very much. I don't know what I would do without you in my life." I kissed both of them and then said, "Wynona, until I leave this house, I don't want to hear one word come out of your mouth; not one fuckin word."

I packed my bags and was walking out. Willow and Angel saw me leaving and began to cry. I explained that I would always love them but it was time for me to put a lot of space between their mother and I. I told Willow I would come by tomorrow and pick her up so she could go over to the hospital to see her brother. I kissed them on they're forehead and Willow cried even louder as I walked out the door. She told her mother it was all her damn fault and said she hated her. I didn't look back.

I called my dad and told him my situation; he gave me his address and told me to come to his house. What he didn't know was his address had been in my wallet for years. That's when it dawned on me that I missed my meeting with Mr. Hutchens. I placed a call to his office and got his voice mail. I left my message about my son and my medical emergency, and asked him to return my call as soon as he could. As I drove up to the house my dad's front door opened; he was standing there waiting. I was overcome with emotion. I couldn't believe my dad and I were actually going to be living under the same roof. He put his hand on my shoulder and said, "Welcome home son." Wow!

His house was so neat and clean it was unreal. I started ginning, my dad said, "Is everything ok?"

I said, "Everything is great"!

We sat and talked for hours. I told him all that I had went through over the years and the new discovery about his grandchildren. I told him I would always love them as my own. It was crazy how my wife and mother had the same characteristics and how he and I fell into the same trap. His eyes filled with tears as he apologized for not fighting harder to get custody of me. I told him everything was fine, I was here now and I was glad he opened his home to me. My dad's steps were slow but I was glad the creator allowed me to finally spend time with him.

A few days later Mr. Hutchens returned my call and asked if I was alright. I told him I was out of hot water now and doing much better. We made arrangements for him to come over to the house to talk and pick up the package I had for him. After I got off the phone dad asked, "Was that Doug Hutchens you were talking to just now?"

I said, "Yes, how did you know?"

"I know Doug very well; he's a good man and a very good reporter. He was at the bar with you that night you got a little too happy. Come and sit down for a second son, we need to talk."

I walked over and sat down on the couch next to him. He said, "Do you remember me telling you that I had something important to discuss with you while you were in the hospital?"

I said, "Yes."

"Well the guy I've had watching you for me brought me surveillance footage of someone else that's been watching you and told me that you were in danger because of something you're doing on your job. We know who's watching you and everyone who's connected with them. I wish you had come to me with this but it's too late now. This meeting you've scheduled with Mr. Hutchens, are you sure you want to continue with this?"

"Dad, I am beyond sure. You don't know what's going on in the detention center and I plan to bring the whole thing down. Between them and Wynona, I can't take any more of it, and those guys in there deserve much better."

"Well if you're gonna do this you'll need help and I got the right people for the job. With what I'm about to tell you I need you to keep your head and stay calm; do you understand?"

"Yeah, sure dad."

"The accident your son was in was no accident; it was a planned attack to send a message to you to get you to stop your investigation of the detention center. Your decision to do what you're doing was way over your head but we have it under control. What I need you to do is complete your meeting with Mr. Hutchens and let him take to ball from there. With the amount of evidence you have there's more than enough to shut the facility down and bring justice to the men you want to help. I'm proud of you for stepping up son; now focus on your family and be happy ok."

Somewhat in shock from what I just heard I somehow got the word "Ok" out of my mouth. How could I have been so foolish to think that no one would notice what I was doing? I was careful with all the cameras around but I forgot about the hidden cameras they told us about that existed. Only a few knew where they were. Whatever dad had done and was doing kept me safe so I followed his instructions exactly.

Mr. Hutchens arrived on time and I explained everything that I had witnessed and showed him all the evidence I had thus far. He could hardly believe what he was seeing and assured me that he would expose these crimes personally. I thanked him for coming by then he and dad walked off a talked for a few minutes. I was still sort of in a daze; was this really happening? Was I really the cause behind Michael almost being killed? The anger was beginning to rise in me again but I promised my dad that I would remain calm. I just hope that Kevin didn't have anything to do with the attempt on my son's life.

Two weeks after I had come home from the Hospital my phone rang and to my surprise it was Crystal. I didn't know whether to answer it or let it go to voice mail. I waited until the very last moment and I picked up. I hesitated, I said, "Hello."

Crystal said, "Ervin, how are you?" Before I could say anything Crystal said, "Ervin I'm not calling as your Doctor, I'm calling as your friend."

"I'm fine."

"Are you sure?"

"No, I'm not sure but I'll be ok."

"Ervin, can I meet you somewhere or can you come to my home, we really need to talk."

I thought about it for a split second, I was no longer in the house so I could go wherever I wanted to. I reluctantly said, "I can come over if that's cool with you." I was so embarrassed to have to face her because she knows my entire life history now, but she was the lady I was in love with. What could she possible want with me? We agreed to meet at five. That way I could help dad out and make sure he ate and was relaxing before I left. My dad was so special to me but I noticed his steps were getting slower and slower every day. I wanted to ask if there was a problem but he didn't seem to be in any pain so I brushed it off to him just being tired.

I told my dad I was going out for a little bit. He asked was I going to visit the children. I said no I was going to go visit my lady friend. His eyebrows did a little dance as he smiled at me.

"I guess I won't wait up for you then."

"Ok dad there you go, it's not like that. Crystal called and said she wants to meet with me."

Dad said, "Now just how cute is that, you two love each other but everything is off limits. Son, soon all of that will change and you and Crystal can build a future together, if that's what you really want to do."

I smiled at the thought of building a future with Crystal. Who would ever think the girl I first had sex with may be my future wife.

"From that smile on your face I take it I'm right. Go ahead and have fun, I'll hold it down till you get back son."

"Thanks dad."

I shaved for a change, put on a nice shirt, a pair of slacks, my head was bald and I even put on a hint of cologne. So fresh and so clean clean! As I drove, the thought of being with Crystal began to grow in me but I was also concerned with what it was she wanted to talk to me about. Did it have anything to do with my mental state or something else? I pulled up to Crystal's house right at five. I walked up to the door and just as I was ringing the bell she answered the door.

"Hey Ervin come on in."

Crystal had on a brown skirt, beige blouse and a nice pair of heels, she was looking nice. She offered me a glass of wine. I asked her would that affect the medicine I was taking. She giggled a little, "No, it shouldn't, it's not like you're going to be drinking the entire bottle."

She had a valid point so I said, "Yes, I would like to have a glass."

She asked, "Chardonnay ok?"

I said, "That will be fine."

Crystal sat down on the opposite end of the couch and took several sips of chardonnay. The way things were going I started getting a little nervous. She began to speak, "Thanks for coming. I picked up the phone several times to call you but I couldn't bring myself to do it."

That statement really made me nervous so I said, "What made you call today?" I turned so I could look at Crystal's eyes, I wanted her to know she had my full attention.

"You and I have been friends for so long I couldn't see not calling to check on you."

"Ok but you could've asked that over the phone."

"Ervin, please let me do this my way ok?"

"I'm sorry let me sit back and relax, go ahead I'm listening."

"Thank you Ervin! I realized some time ago your marriage was in trouble but I didn't want to come between you and your wife. I knew that there was something special between us but I knew I couldn't act on it as much as I wanted to. I'm sorry it ended up like this, I hope that you're ok."

"Crystal it's going to take time but I'm better. I moved out or should I say she asked me to get the bleep out. I've been living with my dad."

"What!, Ervin your dad, Oh my God for real?"

"Yes and it has been amazing! The two of us have been sharing a lot with each other. He's truly a good man Crystal and I'm glad that I was given the opportunity to get to know him. He knows about you too!"

Crystal looked at me with those piercing eyes, "What does he know about me?"

I smiled and said, "Let's just say he knows how I feel about Crystal Foster."

"Ok, well how do you feel about me?"

"Another time Crystal."

"Ok, we'll come back to that question. How are your children, are they fine as well?"

"They can't wait to move away. Wynona has been playing them like pawns to get me to come over."

"Are you thinking of going back?"

Before I knew it I said, "Hell no! I'm finished with that hoe and I'm not looking back. Crystal, I have something else I need to share with you. That night you saw me at the hospital, I only told you half of the truth."

Her eyebrows raised, she said, "Go ahead I'm listening." She took another sip of her chardonnay and so did I.

"My son was in an accident and the reason he had that accident was because he was following his mother. She was going into a bar on the other side of town."

"Ok, I don't get it."

"After my son told me where she had gone I went over to the bar and found Wynona having sex with her babies daddy in one of the booths."

"What! Ervin I'm so sorry."

"Before I could do anything I passed out. She then had the nerve to say I had faked a heart attack in front of my daughter. To make matters worse Michael needed a blood transfusion because of the accident and due to my condition I couldn't provide the blood so Willow decided to do it. That's when I found out that Willow nor I was a match for him."

Crystal's mouth flew open, "You're not about to tell me Michael isn't your biological son are you?"

Tears sat on the brim of my eyelids but I refused to cry another tear over that bitch! I slowly shook my head yes, "Crystal, Michael nor Willow are my biological children."

Crystal jumped up and said, "What! You got to be fucking kidding me. Ervin, why didn't you tell me this at the hospital?"

"I couldn't, I felt if I had told you any more I would've exploded and looking at your reaction you might have done the same thing. With all of this on me and the thought of losing you and the children, it was just too much. It was enough that I share part of my story; I wanted to survive. There's more but I think it best that I wait to tell you about it. I'm looking to rebuild my life one step at a time. How long have you been working at Columbia Memorial?"

"About that, I'm working there on call and I have my own private practice. I'm doing that until I build up enough clients to fly solo."

"I was so shocked to see the door swing open and it was you."

"When I got the record and I looked at the name I didn't associate it to you because there's always more than one person with the same name, however, when I opened the door and saw you I actually panicked for a second; then I kicked into Dr. Foster mode. I knew I could handle it although it was a challenge because for real I was supposed to walk back out the door and say it was a conflict of Interests."

"Why didn't you?"

"From the look on your face Ervin I knew you needed me and I wasn't about to let you down. I think it hurt more after I left out of the room because my best friend was truly hurting and I didn't know. How could I not know? I had to run into the break room and grab a cup of tea and calm myself down; I couldn't lose focus on the problem. How is your mother doing?"

"Well she wrote me a letter saying why she treated me so horrific. I haven't written her back yet but I'll get around to it eventually. She's mad as hell right now because I chose to go to my dad's house instead of going to the hoe shack. Crystal you already know there's no way in hell I was ever going to go back to that house and forcing myself to suffer through all the smell of sex and alcohol. I would sleep on the streets before I ever think of going back there."

"You know Ervin, when we were kids I knew your mom had a lot of men coming and going. At one point I wanted to have a lot of men just like her, that is until I slept with you and you dumped me remember?"

Damn, she took a dagger and shoved it straight in my heart, someone please help me pull it out. "Okay, I was hoping that moment would never be spoken of again. We were very young and unwise; neither of us knew what the hell we were doing, however, I do remember you being my first. It felt so damn good."

Crystal looked at me and blushed, we laughed together.

"Every time I thought of you and especially seeing you, that memory always haunted me. The very one that was brought to me, I threw away. Before I make any more mistakes let me take this opportunity to say I apologize for how I treated you. I promise you it will never happen again. I know this may sound a little ignorant but my goal was to bust as many cherries as I could. I was doing what I saw my brother and mom doing but that didn't make it right. I really feel bad about having done that to you."

"Ervin listen, I was just as hot as you were. I wanted the experience remember? I said at one point I wanted all the boys too but after a few swings and going away the next summer to my aunt's house, I learned a huge lesson about my essences. I Buckled down and started to take my studies seriously and I stopped thinking about sex and men altogether.

Ok, let me get to the reason I called you over to my house. Ervin, I have spent a great deal of time alone and I have prayed and prayed for God to bring me my Prince. The last time we were together you told me you were letting me go so I could find a suitor and start my life. Well I came to the conclusion that you have always been my life. Even though it happened only once, that moment with you captured my heart and I have never desired to be with anyone else like I do with you. Ervin, I will wait as long as

I have to because I know in my heart I want to spend the rest of my life with you."

I slowly sat up straight, the tears building in my eyes; (Yes I'm a grown ass man but I'm an emotional creature as well. "You Punk ass, I'll let it go this time.") I guess the smile on my face was enough to tell what I felt but I had to tell her what has always been in my heart for her. "Crystal, I knew from the very first moment I saw you that there was something special about you. I tried over the years to act as if I didn't feel anything but the more I saw you the more it was evident that you were the princess I needed in my life. I made some unwise and hasty decisions back then so I had to live with it. Marrying Wynona was a huge mistake and it cost me many years. Willow and Michael came and it changed my entire world. Because of what I have gone through, I refuse to allow my children to grow up without a father. I know I've been scared and broken from living in a dysfunctional family but I had to do my best to make sure my children had a better life than me. I am honored and relieved to know that you feel as you do. Crystal, I'm in love with you and have always been. Although I haven't touched you since I was a youth, the burning you left in me then has never gone away."

I know I have some deep rooted issues from my past that I must continue to work through. With you by my side I have no doubt that I'll be more then fine. I need you Crystal, I have always needed you. You are my best friend and I know if we continue to allow God to work with us this beautiful friendship we share will flourish into something beyond anything we could ever imagine, as long as we put him first in everything we do."

I got up and moved closer to her and put my arms around her; she still smelled like and exotic honeysuckle. I allowed the scent to flow in my nostrils and fill my soul; it felt like heaven was opening up. I looked at her with those deep piercing eyes and kissed her with such tenderness. She returned a kiss of such passion that it overwhelmed me. A tremendous surge rushed through me like never before. Mini Me practically jumped through my pants, I couldn't dare let Crystal see how intoxicating she made me feel. My lifelong dream of the day we would embrace and become one was finally becoming reality.

"Crystal, I learned from one of my dad's friends that when a man and woman come together for the first time, and the woman opens her sacred flower and offers her precious ring to him; the moment he accepts her ring and enters into her eternal love they become one spiritually; husband and wife. So we have technically been married a long time." We both smiled at each other and sat back on the couch making plans for our future. I promised to make good on what I was saying.

Chapter 15

"Hey dad, how are you today? I noticed you don't seem to be feeling like yourself, is there anything I can do?"

"How are things with you and Crystal?"

"Things are great but don't avoid my question."

My dad looked sad; we had been getting along so well. He encouraged me to see a counselor along with just clearing my head from all the bull shit. My dad asked me to go with him to the doctors so I told him sure why not. I wanted to make sure he was ok.

On the way to the VA Hospital my dad started to explain to me when he was in Vietnam he had gotten exposed to Agent Orange. I racked my brain while I drove to remember what agent orange was then it popped in my head that agent orange was a powerful mixture of chemical defoliants that the government supposedly used during the war to eliminate forest cover. From dad's explanation, it turns out that the real purpose for this poison called a chemical was as a biological weapon to kill the enemy. Unfortunately before it was used on the enemy they used the troops as guinea pigs to see how it worked.

Those directly exposed had severe reactions and died. Those who came in contact with the poison from being in the jungle suffer for years before most succumb to its designed end.

Then I hear my father say, "I have a tumor in my brain and it's not getting any smaller, and a nasty rash on my back that goes along with it. I've done good all these years and now this. You're right, I am slowing down and I think it has something to do with the tumor. So today I'm seeing my doctor once again to see what stage I'm in."

I was driving and trying to comprehend what my dad was saying; what stage of Agent Orange. My heart started beating wildly and my hands were gripping the wheel so tight I thought it might break. My dad looked over at me, he said, "Son you ok?"

I shook my head yes. "I'm fine." I was coming out of one tragedy moving into another. Is this what they mean about trials and tribulations and picking up your own cross and walking? I don't understand why the good people always seem to be punished. What did I do to deserve this? Why my father?

We made it to the VA and signed in. It seemed like they had been waiting on my dad because we didn't even get a chance to sit down before they called him. This was my first time actually being in the VA; it looked more like a college campus then a hospital. The only difference was that it was full of old people. I had never seen a hospital with nothing but old people in it before and no one smiled or seemed happy about anything. It really made me feel weird.

Shortly after the attendant showed us to the exam room Dr. Yim came in and greeted us. "How are you doing today Mr. Wyatt?"

"Well I'm feeling ok at the moment but I've been better."

"Have there been any changes in your condition since your last visit?"

"Not much, just moving a little slower these days."

"Dad you're moving a lot slower then you were. In just the last 30 days you have slowed down quite a bit and I've been concerned but just didn't say anything."

"Well doc that's my reason for coming in today. I wanted to know what else can be done or what I should expect from this point."

"From what you have told me today I see things have progressed more rapidly than I was expecting. If you recall from your last visit I talked to you about the advanced stages of Agent Orange poisoning and the affects it has on certain organs and systems of the body. With this latest information it appears that your condition has accelerated beyond a point that we can do anything about."

"So how long do I have doc?"

"Well it's difficult to know for sure but I would safely say about 18 months."

Almost the whole ride home was in silence. I was speechless and didn't know how to say what was going through my mind. I was angry but couldn't let my dad see me cracking up; I didn't want to cause him any more pain. That's when this great calm came over me and I decided that I'd make the next eighteen months the best he ever had. I had enough saved up to handle things for a long while so I decided to turn all my evidence over to DOJ and quit my weekend job at the detention center. My supervisor at the plant was very understanding and changed my schedule to 3 days per week with no change in pay. I tell you, when the Lord blesses He really blesses.

My children and I spent every moment we had with my dad after I explained to them that his time was coming to a close. Willow and Michael both were at the house almost every day to see their Papa, as they affectionately called him. They played games with him, read stories and when he would drift off to sleep from the medication they would sit right there waiting for him to open his eyes again. He shared some stories with them about his trips abroad. He told them how special I was and that they should always keep me close. A few times both children would be overcome with emotion so much so that there wasn't a dry eye in the house.

I took it upon myself to invite the children over for a special dinner. There was a few things I wanted to talk to them about. Crystal and I decided that she should be there when I told the children of my discovery almost 5 months ago. I didn't want to wait on Wynona's getto ass to tell them a half truth; I wanted them to know the real truth. After they arrived I explained to them that Crystal was my woman now and would be there for the rest of our lives. While dad was upstairs resting I sat the children down and as nervous as I was, Crystal holding my hand, I told them first that Crystal and I had been friends since we were children and that we were going to be married as soon as the divorce was final. She helped me take care of my father and she also helped take care of me.

Willow spoke first, she said, "Dad, I'm so happy for you; you deserve to have some type of happiness." Michael was slow to speak but he said he understood that life moves forward and I truly deserved to be happy. He wondered where that would leave him and Willow.

"Well that's the next thing I want to talk to both of you about. You know that I love you and my feelings for you will never change, however, 5 months ago when you were in the hospital I found out that neither of you are my biological children as a result of your need for a blood transfusion. After it was learned that Willow wasn't a match I asked the Dr. what your blood type was and he told me A-. This immediately meant that I wasn't a match either because I have 0+ blood. Final confirmation of this fact came when Angel turned out to be a match for you.

"So dad what you're saying is if you and Willow couldn't give me blood we're not related."

"Yeah sorta; You, Willow and Angel may have the same father but I'm your dad, just not your biological father. I want you to know that I'll always be your dad because I raised all of you and no matter what anyone says, you're my children. I will always be here for you; I needed to tell you this before someone came out and tried to tell you a half truth.

Willow said, "Now what you're saying is you didn't want mom to come up and tell us a damn lie on top of all the other lies she has told us over the years. Dad I'm sorry, we took a lot of shit off our mom. Don't get me wrong, I believe what the bible says about honoring your mother and father so that our days are longer but my mom has never really been here for me and I'm sick at the thought that someone else is my father. You're my father! You always have been and always will be." Crystal squeezed my hands as if she was proud of me. I got up and hugged both my children. Michael was taking this harder than I thought he would; holding his feelings in.

Crystal stood up and asked Willow if she would come to the kitchen and help her get some tea. Willow said sure and off they went. Michael and I stood quiet then he said, "Dad that's my mom, she had me so why would she lie about who she slept with; what did you do to her that she didn't love you."

"Son I have asked myself that same question for years and I still don't have an answer. You've been watching for years yourself and you know my routine; I went to work and came home to take care of you every day. You even took it upon yourself to find out what she was doing so the spirit was telling you something was wrong. There are things I can't explain son but what I do know is I have always been here for you and that will never change."

"Dad I love you and my mom, it's going to take me some time to get passed this because it's like, who am I; what kind of man will I be. Will I end up like my mom bitter and confused? I watched you over the years trying to be a good husband but nothing was ever good enough for her. Do you think she'll ever tell us the truth?"

"Son again, I can't answer for your mom; all I know is I can't live a lie."

Cyratal and Willow entered with drinks; they were all smiles. "Dad, Crystal's going to take me to get my nails done and get my eyebrows arched; that's if you approve."

I smiled and said. "Sure, you're old enough to make your own decisions, just don't let it go to your head." We all laughed. We ended our evening with dinner and a movie Papa in the middle; he was having a good evening for a change. I fought back tears as I watched them all together around my dad. I will never forget this moment.

Crystal and I had some alone time after I made sure my dad was comfortable. She told me I did a great job telling my children the truth about who I was to them. I was glad and thanked her for being there for me.

She said she wanted to stay the night with me; she had been coming daily to help out but tonight was different. I saw something different in her eyes, the same light piercing eyes were there but they were magical this time; they looked as if they were dancing. I asked if she was sure because I didn't want to taint what she believed in; she had been faithful to her church and herself. She put her finger to my lips and led me to my room.

I had a Mahogany canopy style bed; it set up high off the floor as you entered the room. I stood still and watched her take off her clothes. I instantly flashed back to our youthful days; standing before me was a true princess. She had small beautiful breasts that stood up firm for a woman in her early 40's. Her stomach was flat, thighs and legs were very well toned; hell the only thing that was different was she was older and more developed. She removed her bra and panties and stood there for me to take it all in. I walked up to her, slowly ran my hands over her body, pulled her to me and kissed her ever so passionately. The love flowing through me was as if I was pouring myself into her and her into me. She sighed like it was a big relief to feel my lips upon hers. I cupped her breast and gently kissed them one at a time. I sucked each nipple as she started to moan ever so lightly. I looked into her eyes, picked her up and laid her on the bed. My clothes melted away as I climbed onto the bed with her.

"May I take my time with you tonight my love?"

Her soft voice said, "Time stands still for you my baby."

As I slowly caressed her body I could feel the heat rising all over her. Minnie Me was standing at full attention screaming, "Dive, dive." I caressed and licked her body until I found her secret place. My tongue slowly passed through her pussy lips, tasting her sweet nectar as my tongue found its way to her clit. I sucked it as it stood at attention, gentle firm strokes with two fingers inside as she begged me for more. Her back arched in full acceptance of the love I was ravishing her with. I wanted her so bad but I had to savor every moment because I wanted her to know I loved her and this was the beginning of us officially becoming one. Feeling her climax again she said she couldn't wait any longer; she rolled me over, climbed on top and slowly let my dick sail deep into her caramel valley. The way her muscles clung to me and slowly stroked up and down took my breath away. He body moved like liquid fire as she stared deep into my soul and milked every drop of cream from me. We made love all night long, never tiring or wanting to stop.

"You know we have a lot of catching up to do but I don't want to hinder you or your values my love."

Crystal brushed my lips softly and said, "This is my decision and I know you're my husband, you have always been. I've waited all these years for you so don't go getting philosophical on me. This is the only decision I could make and from what I see I'm right where I want to be; with the man I've always loved."

I lay with her in my arms and let those words sink in for a few minutes. When you say you love someone you must truly know what those words mean. I knew Crystal could start a sentence or thought and I could finish it; when she walked near my heart would jump and my body would be set ablaze. Her mindset was where I needed it to be. I knew she loved me before tonight and her eyes let me see the glow she had around her; it was love indeed. I was ready to tell her that she completed me; she always helped me be the best I could be. Instead of finding fault she helped me conquer my fears. When she kissed me I thought I was in paradise; the slightest touch from her was enough to calm the storm that raged within. No one else had this effect on me and I wanted her to have my fire; I wanted to be the one who would continue to let her blossom beyond the heavens. Then I rolled over and looked into her eyes, "I have loved you for a very long time and yes I know at one point it was wrong to have those feelings but they were real. I'll do everything in my power to be the man you've desired to spend the rest of your life with." We kissed and embraced each other until we fell asleep under the moon light.

We woke up the next morning and to our surprise my dad was down stairs waiting. We looked at each other and smiled. Dad greeted us with, "It's about time you two playmates got up, I'm hungry; actually I'm starving."

Crystal went into the living room and kissed the top of my dad's head and asked what he wanted to eat. He smiled up at her and said, "Anything those pretty little hands will fix for an old man like me." I slowly walked into the living room looking at my dad, there was something different, he seemed to be at peace today; no pain, no worries, he seemed happy. I sat down and asked him was it hard for him to get down the steps.

He said, "No, actually I walked down the steps better than I've done in months." He leaned in and said, "Did you two finally retie the knot."

I actually blushed at the question; I hesitated for a few seconds then said, "Yes we loosed the fire that was there from years ago."

"Good, you needed to feel her positive energy."

I looked in the kitchen at Crystal, she pretended not to be listening but I knew she was; she looked up at me and smiled. I love that damn woman and I wanted everyone to know just how I felt.

After breakfast dad said he wished to speak to me alone. Crystal said that was fine, she was on her way to the office for a couple hours and I was off today. I walked her to the door and she said, "I wonder what the talk will be about?"

I kissed her soft lips and said, "I'll fill you in on all the details when you come back. You are coming back right?"

She looked at me and said, "I wouldn't miss the encore for nothing in the world," then she slyly put her hand on my dick and pouted out her lips for another kiss. Shiiiiiiiiiiit, my body instantly caught ablaze. She said, "Momma's gonna take care of that when I get back." I had to stand there and hold on to the door for a minute. My dad was back there cracking up.

When I finally regained my composure, dad quietly sat there for few moments; he must have been gathering his thoughts. "I want to take my three grandchildren on a trip somewhere this weekend, can you make it happen?"

"Dad what about your health, you know what the Dr. said."

"Son, I said I want to take my grandchildren on a trip."

"Ok dad, where do you want to go on such short notice?"

"Anywhere son, anywhere!" His eyes looked like they would spill tears; I didn't want him to cry.

"Ok, I have to work on Sunday but I can get someone to switch with me and then we can leave out on Friday morning, set up in the afternoon, staying all day on Saturday and Sunday then return Monday afternoon. How's that sound?"

"Sounds good Ervin, sounds real good."

I asked him how long he wanted to sit down stairs. He told me he was fine and comfortable for now. I walked away; I didn't know what to make of his sudden change in demeanor but I was going to do as requested.

I called the children and asked them to cancel their plans, and if they had to work I asked them to see if they could have the weekend off as a special request from their ailing grandfather. We planned to take dad up to Kings

Mountain; he loved the scenery, it was so beautifully breathtaking, and the children liked the mountains as well.

The trip was planned and everyone was ready to go; we didn't know what would happen once we got there but we were letting dad lead. We all piled into my dad's SUV; Crystal was in the front seat looking lovely as always, Willow and Michael had their granddad sitting in the middle of them so they could fuss over him and Angel was in the rear seat in his ear. He laughed and sang all the way up the mountains. He dropped off to sleep just before we got there; everyone was quiet and let him rest. This was a lot for him and to have been partially bed ridden to getting up and moving around like nothing was wrong was downright scary. I was hoping my dad wasn't coming up here to dye in the damn Mountains. My sweet princess prepared us all, she said that you never know how these things could work out; we were his closest family and he wanted all of us to be with him.

When I stopped the car dad's eyes popped open like he was a child and said, "Move Michael, let me out." He wanted to take in the sweet air of the mountains. He told the children that between each deployment he would come up to the mountains to do his own detox.

That weekend dad took the children out with him sharing some of his life history. He told them that family is everything and without it you have nothing. He told them to respect their step mother to be and encouraged them to follow their own dreams and aspirations. He told his granddaughters not to have children until they were in love and truly ready for the responsibility of motherhood. He told Michael that if you lay down with fleas you get up with fly's swarming around his manhood. Make sure you take your time and find the right one who respects herself and you. He told each child to build and keep a strong relationship with their dad regardless of the past. Love now and love hard for tomorrow is not promised to any of us.

That evening dad had coffee while sitting on the cabin porch, he asked Crystal to join him. He told her, "You know, I'm preparing to die but before I go I need to know that you'll take care of Ervin. He's been through enough in his life and I just want him to be happy, and if I don't know anything else I know you make him extremely happy."

Crystal assured him that she would never let me go and that she would always be there for me. When I look back at that special weekend, he talked to everyone one on one but me. I was ok but it struck me funny.

On the ride home that Monday afternoon we were all singing and having a wonderful time when a news break came on the radio. We weren't paying much attention to it because we were singing our own songs and didn't have the volume up load. The only part I caught was something about breaking news and detention center. I turned up the volume and listened to the rest of the broadcast.
"...Officials are unavailable for comment at this time but resources have confirmed that at least 12 officers have been indicted on numerous charges including cruel and unusual punishment, rights violations and more. And now for your..."

I turned the radio down and looked back at dad; he smiled and went right back to singing with the children. I'm not sure what he did but I was glad that things worked out for the guys at the center and that justice was finally being served on the real criminals.

It seems as though my life was starting to shift in a good orbit; I woke up the next morning and went down stairs. Dad was in his usual place so I ran back up the steps, my heart skipping beats. I got to the door and knocked lightly saying to myself please let him answer. "Come in," the voice said. I breathed a sigh of relief. I entered and put on a great big smile, "Hey dad how are you feeling today."

"I'm good son."

"I've been up thinking."

"What about?"

"You need me to do something for you?"

He got quiet, "I do have a request of you."

"Ok," I perked my ears up and said, "Shoot"

"Can you please ask your mother to come over here or you go get her?"

I was thinking to myself, "What on earth would he need with her," I was blown away but whatever my dad wanted I was going to make sure he got it. I was going to make sure he did whatever he needed to do.

I made arrangements for my mom to come over to the house; she fussed and cussed saying she didn't need to see no man dying and all drawled up. I told her to please do it for me and my dad. She decided to come over. I was impressed; she was dressed nicely, had on a wig that was civil and not wild, she smelled good and she looked nice for a change. I helped her move up the steps; I could feel as I held her hand to steady her that even her steps were finally starting to get slow but you couldn't tell her ass that, she still thought she was hot shit!

I knocked on the door and dad said come in. I stayed at the door, this was the first time ever and most likely the last time I would see both my parents in the same room together.

Dad said, "Hello Molly, how are you?"

She stood there a moment, she looked like she was paralyzed, then she stuttered and said, "I'm fine Wyatt, why did you ask me to come over here?"

My dad looked up at me and said, "You can leave us son, I got this hell cat." I smiled and shut the door.

I had my reservations as to why he called my mom to his house; he has never wanted or bothered to communicate before now. I was truly puzzled and amazed that she was being half way civil.

Two hours into the visit I knocked on the door, dad said, "Come in, you just couldn't leave us be could you?" My mom was sitting on the bed with her feet propped up. Dad had pictures all over, mom looked embarrassed.

"In a way I thought you two could use something to eat and drink."

My parents looked at each other and broke out laughing. I set the tray down and backed out the door. I couldn't believe my eyes; these two were acting like they were the best of friends. Half hour later my mom tearfully came down the steps. I hurried over to her, "Is everything ok mom?"

"Yes Ervin, he's asleep now. Let Wyatt rest."

I shook my head obeying orders. I stood for a few moments then asked if she was ok.

She looked at me and said, "I'll be ok Ervin. Seeing him helped me finally realize how much of a fool I've been all these years to you and Wyatt, but most importantly to myself." She touched my face and said, "I must go but all is forgiven." She grabbed me and held me tight; this was a first and I didn't want her to ever let go! I walked her to the car, kissed her cheek and said goodbye. Sitting in the living room I was preparing for work; Crystal was going to be coming in soon as she normally sat with dad at night while I worked.

Sure enough Crystal came through the door and to my delight she kissed and hugged me like never before. You already know who was up trying to get a kiss and hug too right? Yep, Minni Me at full attention. I gave her a synopsis of the day; she was intrigued and shocked all in the same breath. I told my future wife I had to run, work was calling but I hadn't forgotten her promise. This time I put my hand between her legs and felt all that goodness flowing with honey. She said, "You keep that up and you won't make it to work tonight, now get."

The next day all was running smoothly when I got home. My dad asked me to come sit with him; he hardly said a word since my mom had come by. He motioned for me to come sit on the bed. I got in the bed and put my arm around him, "Hey dad!"

He had lost so much weight he was now a little big giant. We talked for over an hour about everything then he got silent, he said, "Ervin, one day soon I'm going to leave this earthly place." I moved a little closer and he said, "Sit still son, I need to tell you a few things. I'm ready to go now; I've taken time to visit with all my family members and past friends. You're the most important out of everyone to me. I must thank you and the heavens for you coming into my life; you're a true son. You've brought me more joy in these last few months than I have received all of my life. I want to apologize to you also. Your mom and I had an affair back in the day son and she could swing those hips like nobody's business. Those hips had you screaming for more; sorta like your Crystal. I would meet her once a month and every time I came in town we always had a good time. She would stop whatever she was doing to see me, but what your mom didn't tell me was she was a married lady. I became enraged at the very thought that I was having an affair; I could have been killed. She explained the circumstances to me about Don's dad being gay and that was the only reason she was acting like a jezebel. I offered to marry her and she said she wasn't going to be the marrying kind anymore. She wanted as many men as she could have because they made her feel free and it took all the pain away. I begged a few times but she flat out said hell no so a few years went by and I ran into one of my Army buddies; that's how I learned about you. I asked about her and if anyone had seen her because she stopped coming over to the base. I still had her address so I showed up that very day I first met you and I knew when I saw you that you were mine.

Son, I brought your mother over here to ask for forgiveness for hating her all these years because she kept you away from me. I told her I was prepared to make heaven my home now but before I could take my flight I needed to at least apologies to her. She told me she has always loved me but just didn't want to mess up my life after her first husband scared her the way he did. She felt like there was no man worthy of ever holding her heart again. So son, I've made peace with everyone and now I need you to prepare yourself to let me go. I need to know you'll be happy when I'm gone. I certainly know you've had a rough life but you shall live and be happy; I assure you of this. Just promise me you'll be ok."

I was so choked up with emotion it was hard for me to fathom the thought that my dad was going to leave me. We spoke volumes to each other; I told him I loved him with every fiber in me. I said I didn't want him to suffer but I wasn't ready for him to go either. We embraced and cried. If it was God's will then it shall be; I knew his spirit would always be with me.

About two weeks later my dad passed away in his sleep. The past eighteen months I wouldn't trade for anything in the world. I found my father, I bonded with my father and I gave all my love to my father until he was called home. Seeing him at peace the morning I found him lying there brought an unexplainable joy to me. Crystal came in and hugged me from behind. I smiled and said, "All is well my love, he's finally at peace." I leaned over and kissed his forehead, and then we called for an ambulance.

Going through the house I found a letter addressed to me. I sat down with Crystal and read the letter.

My Dear Son,

If you're reading this that means I have found my way home. As you will soon learn, I have made all the necessary arrangements for you to have a peaceful and happy life for as long as you wish. All that I have belongs to you now and someone from JAG will be contacting you to explain exactly what I mean by this.

I can't tell you how wonderful it has been to finally have you in my life. Although I had to wait, I couldn't have asked for a better son. Watching you grow into the man you are and seeing you with your children has brought unspeakable joy to me. I admire you son, I wish I could have been the man I see in you.

I'm so glad God finally allowed us to come together. If there were ever any doubts of there really being a heaven, these past few months with you have let me see that it certainly does exist. Take care of my grandchildren and let them know that I love them dearly.

P.S.

Tell that Angel of yours, Crystal, that I love her and to take care of you and don't ever let you go for any reason.

I love you both. Just so you know, I'll be watching over you.

Love Dad

My dad may be gone from this world but I feel his spiritual presence all around me. As I put my arms around Crystal I couldn't hold back the tears from streaming down my face. She just held and rocked me for a few moments. She looked up at me and said, "I wouldn't have missed seeing you and your father grow together these last few months for anything in the world. You're an amazing man Ervin, and you're getting stronger every day. Just remember his words and keep God first in everything you do. Yes, it does hurt and you may feel you didn't have enough time with your dad but God planned it perfectly. Cherish and hold the moment close to your heart and remember I'll always be here with you."

That night I went and got my children. Crystal and I informed them that their papa was gone on to a better place. Michael cried first, he told me he knew the time was near; he could feel it was time for papa to leave. He said he was in school thinking about him all the time. Willow sat in silence; I saw the tears build up in her eyes but she didn't let them fall. She told me her mom said that life is not forever and that we live to die; everyone has an appointed time to go. Willow said she hopes she could see her papa and her great granddad Joe again one day, which was my grandpa. I shook my head, took Willow's hand and softly kissed it, and said, "We will see both of them again if we live right." Michael asked could he go to the funeral service. I told them they could most certainly go. Willow slowly shook her head and said, "Momma said when papa dies she didn't want us to go to his funeral." We all sat at the table; I asked each one what did they want to do and they both said in unison that they wanted to attend the funeral service.

I wasn't going to fight with Wynona about what would take place, I knew my children would be there whether she liked it or not.

About a week later Capt. Wilkins from JAG came to the house just as my dad said they would. He explained that my dad had put a very detailed and sophisticated investment plan together specifically for me just after he learned I was born. He also had a trust drawn up and named me as the only beneficiary. All of my dad's earthly possessions, business earnings and investment earnings had been going through this trust. He explained that my dad was the trustee and upon his death that he was named successor trustee.

Everything my dad owned would now come to me. After looking over all the papers presented to me I learned that the investment plan was incredibly large and I actually didn't have to work ever again if I didn't want to. As wonderful as this was, none of those things were what I wanted; I wanted more time with my father. I thanked Capt. Wilkins for coming by and asked that he keep me informed with any matters dealing with the trust.

After my dad's death I finally made up in my mind to walk away and never looked back at Wynona. I could see my children whenever I wanted and that was enough for me. I have and will forever have my dad in my heart. We had taken the time to learn about each other and he even became attached to my children which is a true blessing.

My mom came over and said she wanted to talk to me; I was stunned but allowed her to come in. We went to the study, she paced the floor as if she was nervous. I asked was everything ok.

She said, "No Ervin everything's not ok but it will be...listen. Remember the day your father invited me to come over here?"

I shook my head yes.

"Well we had a long heart to heart talk and I want to explain some things to you. First I want to say that I'm so sorry for the way I treated you throughout your life." She was trying hard not to cry. "You didn't ask to be born into a world of sin; sin that I created. I hated the fact that I carried another man's seed while I fucked around in the streets with whoever I chose. Wyatt asked me to marry him but I couldn't see past the pain Charles caused me so I lost it; I lost me. I thought I was paying Charles back but hell he could care less about who I was fuckin cause he liked dick just as much as I did; he just took it in the ass."

She looked at me and said, "I'm sorry I got carried away. What I'm trying to say son, I realized that I didn't just hurt myself; I hurt you and your father as well. I also want to say that I'm sorry for not coming to you and telling you Wynona was cheating on you. I know you had to find out that the children weren't yours but I promise you I had no way of knowing Mike was doing Wynona until way down the line and I started to put two and two together. I was mad as shit to find out that Mike's old ass was screwin Wynona too. That's the day I came over to the house and told Wynona she needed to tell you. Please forgive me son."

I explained, "Dysfunctional families are everywhere you look but we have to stop and break the mold so it doesn't slip down to the next generation. Yes there are plenty things I can talk about but why, it's water under the bridge. At the end of the day you're my mom, I love and respect you and I have asked god to take the pain away. I appreciate you coming over to tell me how you feel but I let this go a long time ago. The way I see it, I was either going to lose my life or have a heart attack behind other peoples bullshit. Mom, there have been moments the pain was unbearable but the prayers of the righteous held it all together for me; and also for you." I stood there and hugged her tight; she broke loose with tears streaming down her face, she said, "You don't know what these words mean to me son."

As time moved on I sat down and wrote my mom a letter to apologize for the incident that took place at the hospital. I told her I was so caught up emotionally that I had to ask for forgiveness as well. I told her god gives us one mother; regardless of how she treated me I still loved her and that I appreciated the fact she came to me and had the one on one, it cleared up a lot of pain that burned inside me!

My Grandma has always been a great support system; she continues to love me unconditionally. I know she misses my granddad because I sure do. I can still hear him saying, "Son, what's on your mind, how are you living, is everything ok?" She was coming over just as much if not more than the children were. My Grandma was lonely and concerned; sometimes she would have me pick her up and other days she would just show up. She said she had to check on her grandson. It made me feel good to know I was loved. She told me she knew God wouldn't put more on me than I could bare. She hinted that I should look at building my relationship with God for he was the reason I was still here. Grandma also knew losing Grandpa and my dad was a lot to handle as I loved them both dearly. I know she was just concerned about me and I was just as concerned about her; she lost her only love and best friend. She asked about my relationship with Crystal and I explained that I had a plan in motion to ask her to be my wife but I wanted it to be special.

She smiled and said, "I see a glimmer of hope and love in those pretty brown eyes."

I smiled even deeper; Yeah, Crystal did that to me, she moved me in ways Wynona couldn't or wouldn't. I sat down with my coffee in hand and told her, "Crystal loves the lord and I want to surprise her by showing up at church and start attending but I don't want to go because it's the right thing to do, I want to go and have peace restored to my life along with building my personal relationship. As I looked at my Grandma I didn't know from day to day when her last day would come but until then I wanted her to be proud of me. She had always been my main source of support.

After a few short weeks and time alone I realized everything was done for the best. I started refining my relationship with God and found peace.

I took time to see the errors that was made in my relationship and didn't wish no bad luck on Wynona but I knew no good would come of the way she treated me.

My children would call every week saying they couldn't wait to leave home. Their mother was trying to use them as pawns to get me over to the house. They didn't want any part of what their mom was doing. They also told me how Wynona was seeing her old boyfriend. She would always be dressed like one of those street women, everything was tight, she was showing too much cleavage, had on way to much makeup and she was drunk most of the time. I would just shake my head. I told the children they were always welcome to come home whenever they were ready.

Life for me was better than I could have ever imagined it would be. I decided to listen to my princess's request and retire. She felt I had worked damn hard for a lot of years and it was time for me to relax and do something I wanted to do. I started my own little business. I opened my own electronics store fully equipped with all the latest toys. I was so happy my life couldn't have been better. My children are happy and doing very well; they have Crystal and I in their lives forever.

Crystal's business has flourished as a therapist. After the divorce was final Crystal and I got married six months later. We didn't have a big lavish wedding; something very small and personal. We decided because we were already spiritually married we didn't need to go overboard, however, we did sail away to the Caribbean for two weeks soaking up the sun and making love. She's my soul mate; there is no doubt in my mind. While on vacation Michael ran the electronics shop and kept me informed with all the details. He was a good store manager. I was so happy he made the decision to come and work with me.

Michael was a momma's boy; he forgave her for her wrong doings and said she had been real sick lately. He had taken her to the hospital twice; I felt sorry for her because time wasn't standing still. I just hoped she was making peace with herself and God.

My Willow was in college and enjoying life. She didn't come around much but she did stay in contact with me; she was my special daughter. Angel was doing well and was working as an administrative assistant for some big wig downtown. From what I heard, her and her mom had a bigger falling out and she decided to keep her distance; but she called home periodically to check on me and Crystal.

Oh yeah, it turns out that Kevin did get caught up in the detention center case that went down and even the guys that tried to take Michael from me ended up getting caught and charged with attempted murder as well. Because the evidence gathered was so compelling and exposed so many people, the case is still ongoing. Many of the inmates have been released because of the violations committed against them; I think as an effort to keep the city from being sued but that really hasn't stopped some of them.

One thing is for sure, I feel good in body and mind. I learned to live, let go of the past and move forward; always keeping God first. I don't harbor any ill feelings about Wynona anymore.

Guess what else; Crystal and I are expecting our first bundle of joy soon. We're told it's twins and praying that we're blessed with one of each so we can be finished. Crystal is 45 and I don't want to put her through the stress of doing this more than once if she doesn't want to. The children are very excited that they'll have little brothers or sisters joining the family. I couldn't be more proud at the thought; I know these are my children. I can feel dad and Grandpa looking down from heaven smiling.

People come into your life for a reason and in a certain season. But then there are those that have always been in your life, that one who was created and born specially for you, your soul mate. If we would only take our time and listen to the spiritual guidance that is always there and not lean on our own understanding, your sparkling Crystal will appear right before your very eyes.

This life with Crystal and I is perfect and we know love flows from heat to heart. Who would have ever thought things would end up this way. I can finally truly say I know how it is to feel love and to be in loved.

I'm glad God allowed me to go through everything I have; it made me a stronger man, father and a true best friend.

("Just because things is all good now, don't think I ain't still here NIGGAH's. Aaaa hahaha!")

Message from the author:

What makes us push those buttons to see the other side of a good man? No, don't pretend you don't know what buttons I'm talking about. You remember; say, say; excuse me mister man; uh hello; I know you hear me talkin' to you; no you gonna listen to me; you ain't shit; make me get out yo face… Well, when the other side of midnight emerges, don't scream, be happy for what you asked for. He breaths fire and can explode at any time, which makes him uncaring, crazy, harsh, bitter, and mean as hell. Why, because you chose to push those buttons and challenged him as a man; the only way out is through you.

We (women) have him (our man) thinking he ain't worth shit and that we'll never be submissive. We walk around trying to be controlling, nagging; a real bitch. We even ration out sex like it's a commodity for the highest bidder. This alone will send most men running into the arms of another woman but yet we say we love him. What part of this is true love to you? Do we actually know a good man when we see one? THERE'S SOMETHING SPECIAL ABOUT A GOOD MAN! He can be hard to find if you're playing the hard bitch role but once you have him do whatever it takes to BE A GOOD WOMAN and keep him. Search yourself and be a real woman at all times. Always do the right thing and never use or abuse him because if you do you just may be the one who wakes up to find yourself alone.

OTHER GREAT BOOKS BY THE AUTHOR

Why I Kept My Past a Secret!

Now That The Secrets Are Out!

Living Free Of The Secrets!